Dear Romance Reader,

Welcome to a world of breathtaking passion and never-ending romance.
Welcome to *Precious Gem Romances*.

It is our pleasure to present *Precious Gem Romances*, a wonderful new line of romance books by some of America's best-loved authors. Let these thrilling historical and contemporary romances sweep you away to far-off times and places in stories that will dazzle your senses and melt your heart.

Sparkling with joy, laughter, and love, each *Precious Gem Romance* glows with all the passion and excitement you expect from the very best in romance. Offered at a great affordable price, these books are an irresistible value—and an essential addition to your romance collection. Tender love stories you will want to read again and again, *Precious Gem Romances* are books you will treasure forever.

Look for fabulous new *Precious Gem Romances* each month—available only at Wal★Mart.

Kate Duffy
Editorial Director

KISSING CAITLIN

Michelle James

ZEBRA BOOKS
Kensington Publishing Corp.

http://www.zebrabooks.com

ZEBRA BOOKS are published by

Kensington Publishing Corp.
850 Third Avenue
New York, NY 10022

First Printing: November, 2000
10 9 8 7 6 5 4 3 2 1

Printed in the United States of America

To my mom, who taught me to dream;
To Cindy Scott, who always brightens my day;

and

To Hilary Sares, who made this book a reality.

Thank you.

Chapter One

Brent Stewart was exactly the man she needed, Caitlin Rogers realized with a start. Funny how she'd never even considered him until this very moment, and now he seemed like the perfect solution to her problem.

Best of all, after knowing him practically all of her life, she knew Brent would do a great job because he was a great guy. No way would he let her down. Not her buddy. Not reliable Brent.

Take right now. Even though it was going to cost his team the game, Brent was protecting her from the dual mountains she called brothers. She'd heard him tackle her older brother, Tony, a second ago, right before she would have gotten tackled herself. Not many guys would do something like that, lose a game to protect a lady. But that was the kind of man Brent was—chivalrous, kind, thoughtful.

P-E-R-F-E-C-T.

Now all she had to do was convince him he was perfect for the job. But if she explained her situation carefully, maybe threw in a couple of pretty-pleases, there was a good chance he'd agree. After all, he'd just moved back to town, so surely he'd want to get involved with the community. What better way to get involved than by taking over her grass-roots volunteer organization, Good Neighbors?

She hoped Brent would see it that way. A whisper of doubt entered Caitlin's mind. Okay, sure, there was a possibility—a remote possibility—that he might say no. She had to be realistic. Stepping up to run a volunteer organization was a major time commitment. Brent really might say no.

Which would be an unbelievable shame. Brent would be terrific as the head of Good Neighbors. He was kind. Smart. Organized.

And sexy as all get out. Not that it had anything to do with the job, but Caitlin would be lying if she didn't admit she'd like to spend the next few weeks looking at him.

She was only human, after all.

No two ways about it, since he'd returned to town she'd been all aflutter. Too bad he wanted to settle down in the very town she couldn't wait to leave. Otherwise she might be tempted to see what kind of mischief she could create with Brent.

But that wasn't going to happen, which was for the best, Caitlin decided as she made it across the makeshift goal line and whooped her victory. A man like Brent might try to change her mind about leaving town. Not that she would. She was much too determined for that. No way was she going to miss this opportunity.

Caitlin's younger brother, Al, ran across the goal line, stopping mere inches from her. As always in the spontaneous football game the four of them played, Al was her teammate. "Can you believe it?" he asked, slapping Caitlin's hand. "We won!"

"We are the best!" With another whoop, Caitlin slammed the ball into the ground and was all set to launch into a victory dance when she caught sight of Tony standing toe to toe with Brent, reading him the riot act.

"That doesn't look good," Al muttered. "If they don't break it up, I'll have to arrest them." He trotted off toward the fighting men.

With a sigh, Caitlin followed. Since Tony was the elementary school principal and Brent was a cop, they knew better than to let their argument get out of hand. But as Caitlin drew closer, she realized Tony really was furious with Brent. Her big brother hated losing, so she wasn't surprised he'd gone ballistic.

Apparently, Al's idea of breaking up the fight was standing on the sidelines and laughing. Resigned, Caitlin took things into her own hands. Rushing over, she stepped between her brother and Brent, the top of her head barely reaching each man's chin.

"Hey, you guys. Enough with the testosterone." She shoved on Tony's chest, moving him only a few inches. "You don't want to get arrested, do you?"

"He tackled me. I had you. I was all set to get you, and he ruined it," Tony hollered. "Dammit, Brent, we're on the same team."

"You were going to ram her, you idiot," Brent said loudly. "Do you have any idea how big you are? How little she is?" He glanced down at Caitlin, his handsome face tense. Caitlin met his gaze, but after a few seconds, looked away. Yikes, the man was good-looking with a capital *good*.

"I'm not exactly little," she pointed out. "I'm almost five-eight."

"Yeah. She's almost five-eight." Tony patted her on top of her head. "For a girl, she's a giant. An Amazon."

Caitlin frowned at her older brother. "I am not a giant, you nitwit."

"But you're not a shrimp, like Brent's making you out to be," Tony said. He gave her a bear hug, and she forced herself not to wince when his grip became a little too enthusiastic. "She's a tough girl and can take it."

Brent muttered a curse. "First, she's not a girl. Tomorrow she's twenty-six." He glanced again at Caitlin, and something in his look made her pulse race a little. Before she could think about the sensation, Brent turned away and continued to talk to Tony.

"Second, she may be five-eight, but she's no match for any of us." Brent moved closer to her brother. "What are you, Tony? Six-four? Six-five? And you outweigh her by about a hundred pounds."

Al moved forward to join the other men, and a loud argument broke out, with each man discussing Caitlin's qualifications to continue participating in these friendly football games. It didn't take long for her to snap. With a groan, she once again pushed against Tony's huge chest, wanting out of this display of masculine idiocy. When the men finally moved back a few feet, she clenched her fists.

"Stop talking about me like I'm not here," she

said with enough force to make all three men fall silent. "I'm not a child."

Tony and Al had the good sense to look shamefaced. She spun to confront Brent, but his direct look sucked some of the fury from her. Funny how much he'd changed during the five years he'd lived in Dallas. For starters, he was much better looking than she remembered. He also had matured, something Caitlin figured her brothers should try.

Yep, Brent had changed. In the old days, he'd treated her like a buddy, a pal, the same way he'd treated her since he'd moved in next door to her family twenty years ago. But now, looking at him, she knew he was different. Just as she was different, she supposed.

She realized suddenly that she didn't really know this man anymore. Maybe that was part of his appeal. She'd noticed the difference in their relationship when he'd first shown up today. He was no longer just good old Brent. Right now, attraction was zapping and zinging around them like fireworks on the Fourth of July.

Almost against her will, Caitlin's gaze skimmed down Brent's broad chest, the muscles well defined under his faded Texas A&M T-shirt. Caitlin's pulse picked up as she studied his large biceps. The bronzed skin gleamed with a sheen of sweat, and Caitlin felt an unfamiliar sensation in her stomach.

With effort, she pulled her attention away from his glorious body and looked at his face. His amazing mocha-brown eyes suddenly seemed so much more intense, more interesting. The same with his darker brown hair, worn short like all the other cops on her father's force. Would his hair feel like silk to the touch? And what about the dark stubble on his chiseled jaw? Would it feel sexy if she ran the tips of her fingers across his cheek?

Yikes. Caitlin closed her eyes and turned away from him. It wasn't as if she hadn't noticed before how handsome he was. She'd known that since the day she'd hit puberty. But before today, he'd always been, well, just Brent. Good old Brent.

Not hunk-a-hunk Brent. Not break-out-in-a-sweat Brent.

Her thoughts were heading in a dangerous direction. She didn't have time to stand here going googoo over the man. She needed his help, that was all. This silly chemical reaction happening between them could mess up everything. If she could find an off switch, she'd flip it. Now was not the time to let her hormones run amok.

When she glanced at Brent again, he met and held her gaze. A blast of desire ran through Caitlin, and she decided she'd better find something else to think about before she embarrassed herself by grabbing Brent and tossing him to the ground. The image made her smile. Like that could happen. She'd have better luck knocking down a mountain.

No, what she needed to do was focus on the problem at hand—getting Brent to agree to take over Good Neighbors. That was all she should be thinking about, not how great he looked with the afternoon sun highlighting his brown hair.

When the men showed no sign of stopping their argument, Caitlin decided to leave the park and head back across the street to her small apartment over her father's garage. Truthfully, she didn't think of her garage apartment as home anymore. In four short weeks, she'd start her job with the Henderson Charity in Dallas; and Desmond, Texas, would be a memory. Finally she'd get to start living her life.

She was halfway across the park when a shrill whistle stopped her. Turning, she saw the men had finally stopped trying to out-macho each other and were trotting over to her.

"Hey, where you going?" Al asked when he reached her side.

"I'm going home," she said, deliberately not looking at Brent.

Tony frowned. "What about the game?"

"The game is over," she said. "Although you and Brent never even noticed, I made the winning touchdown."

Tony's face crumpled in a frown. "Not fair. You two only won because Brent was a jerkface and slammed into—"

"Oh, for crying out loud." Caitlin held up one hand. "Stop. I don't want to hear it again. It's just a game."

As she spoke, she once again became incredibly aware of Brent standing just a few inches away from her. He was close enough for her to smell a hint of the tangy cologne he always wore. But even knowing he was there, she still jumped when he dropped his arm casually across her shoulders and tugged her close for a swift hug.

"I agree," he said. "It's just a friendly game. Let's congratulate Caitlin on her amazing job."

His husky voice made her heart do a funny flitter-flutter. "It wasn't all that amazing," she protested, liking the sensation of him being this close way too much. Drat. Why'd this have to happen now? She hadn't been attracted to a man in a long time. She'd been too busy to fret over her love life. This couldn't happen now. She couldn't let this male-female nonsense get in the way of her plans.

She glanced at Brent. Did he have any idea what he was doing to her equilibrium? What about his own equilibrium? Did he feel the pull between them, or did he still see her as little Caitlin, Tony and Al's sister?

"Sure it was amazing. You're an amazing woman." He grinned down at her, his dark eyes dancing with devilment. His warm, masculine scent surrounded her, tantalizing her, enticing her.

Holy cow.

Brent looked into Caitlin's face and knew he was in big trouble here. Something was wrong. Really wrong. Caitlin was suddenly not the Caitlin he'd always known. This Caitlin was hot. Sassy, shoulder-length black hair, midnight blue eyes. Beautiful. And he could tell from the way she was looking at him, Caitlin felt the same sizzling chemistry he did. Sexual tension arced between them like lightning on a steamy Texas night.

Damn. This was not what he wanted, certainly not why he'd come back to Desmond. He, like everyone else in town, knew Caitlin had plans for her life. Big career plans that included living in Dallas, making a name for herself. She had no room in her life for settling down, and he wasn't interested in a fling.

Idly, he rubbed his side, the small scar still bothering him. Only Dan Rogers, Caitlin's father and his boss, knew he'd been shot six months ago. He'd only been grazed, but it had been his own personal wake-up call. He'd finally admitted to himself he was a small-town cop who didn't like living in the fast lane. And despite what some people thought, Desmond, Texas, really wasn't the end of the earth.

No, Desmond was a great place, a place where he wanted to spend the rest of his life. Sure, there were a few eccentrics in town. And they weren't what you'd call on the leading edge of trends. But Desmond offered exactly the atmosphere he wanted. Slow. Calm. Peaceful.

Of course, he wasn't off to a very good start by getting turned on by a childhood friend. The girl who at ten had taught him to never underestimate a female. The woman who couldn't burn rubber fast enough leaving this town.

Regretfully, he lifted his arm from around Caitlin's shoulders. She gave him a quick, inscrutable glance and then moved away from him. Thank God. He wasn't sure how much longer he could stand there breathing in her seductive perfume and not do something about it.

Tony stepped over and ruffled Caitlin's hair. With a groan, she smoothed it back in place. "Cut it out, bozo," she said, glaring at her brother.

"Sure thing, Caitlin. But what do we do now?" Tony asked. "Give up playing ball just because you turned into a woman?"

An awkward silence fell on the group. Brent watched Caitlin cross her arms across her midriff, but her action only drew attention to her breasts. Full, firm breasts that sent lustful thoughts racing through his mind. He forced himself to look away and study a tree in the corner of the park. He counted to ten. Then twenty. Ah, hell.

"Caitlin can hold her own," Al piped up.

Apparently, she'd had it with their discussion. She muttered something about obnoxious men and started walking toward her father's house again. Brent glanced at his own house, right next door. When his grandmother had died and left it to him, he'd first thought of it as a royal pain. But now he loved that house. Granted, the place needed some work since it had been empty for five years. However, he enjoyed the work . . . every backbreaking second of it.

"Let's go home," Caitlin called over her shoulder. "The rest of the gang should be there by now."

Brent watched the gentle sway of her hips for a moment, then fell into step with Tony and Al, their footsteps crunching the dry summer grass beneath their feet. Caitlin waited for them to catch up to her. Once they had, they made their way slowly, the hot summer sun sapping their energy. More than once, Brent caught Caitlin looking at him, but each time he met her gaze, she abruptly looked away.

Smart move. At least she was fighting this attraction between them. He needed to do the same.

"You know, Caitlin, we can still play football with some of the other guys on the force. They don't care if you're a gir—a woman," Al said, nudging her.

"They should care," Brent muttered. "They could really hurt her." The thought of one of those idiots tackling Caitlin in a football game made Brent's blood pressure rise. "Give it up, Al. It doesn't matter anymore because Caitlin's leaving soon."

He shot her a quick glance. When her gaze caught and held his, his heart slammed in his chest. When had the little girl in pigtails who'd always called him buddy turned into a heartbreaker?

Caitlin felt another shiver of awareness run down

her spine as she looked at Brent. Someone needed to toss ice water on her. Jeez, she was a basket case. This was not the right time to fall for a guy, and Brent was certainly not the right guy to fall for.

With effort, she tried to concentrate on something else. What had her brothers been talking about? Oh, right. Football.

"I think my football days are behind me," she said. "You guys are like mutant monsters. Beside, in four more weeks, I'm out of here. Hang on, Dallas, here I come."

After a brief hesitation, Brent gave her a lopsided grin that made it impossible for her to look away. No wonder women chased him like crazy. He had a way of looking at you that made you think about wild, crazy nights on satin sheets.

Tony snorted. "Figures you'd decide to give up football now, right after you've beaten us."

"We can still play flag with Caitlin," Al suggested.

"Flag? That's for sissies." Tony shook his head in obvious disgust.

"You're just going to have to find a guy to play with," Caitlin said, tired of them acting like babies. "I have other things to think about now."

Thank goodness. Finally she had something to look forward to, something to plan for. These days she was swamped getting ready for the move to Dallas. It was fun. It was exciting. And just as soon as she found someone to take over running the Good Neighbors charity, she'd be home free. The problem was, she didn't feel right asking just anyone. The job was too important. It demanded someone responsible.

Which brought her back to Brent. He really would be the perfect solution to her problem. He wanted to stay in Desmond. He liked the slow pace of the small town. Why else would he leave the excitement and challenge of Dallas?

Seemingly drawn against her will, Caitlin glanced at Brent again. He was watching her carefully, which made her feel flustered. Drat. Where was this chemistry between them coming from? And why'd it have to surface now? She needed Brent to agree to help her with Good Neighbors, not to ask her out.

As they continued walking in the direction of the Rogers's house, Brent asked Al, "How's Madeline?"

"Fine. Tired of being pregnant. But the baby's not due for another three months."

"You excited?"

Al grinned a silly grin. "Yeah. And scared stiff."

They all laughed. Then, Brent said, "Must be a great feeling, becoming a dad. And there's no better place to raise a child than Desmond."

Caitlin wasn't surprised by Brent's words. She'd figured that was why he'd moved back home. He'd sowed his wild oats and now wanted to settle down and start a family. That meant he would be looking for a serious relationship, something that would lead to marriage and children and a life in the two-story brick house his grandmother had left him. The house that sat smack-dab in the middle of the lot next to her father's house.

Well, that ought to squash any attraction she felt for him. Which was just as well. One cold, hard lesson she'd learned from her mother's death was that you didn't always get a second chance to make your dreams come true. By working for the Henderson Charity, she'd not only be able to have her dreams, she'd be helping lots and lots of other people as well.

She couldn't wait.

"You know, Caitlin," Al said. "All of us are against this move you've got planned. I mean the whole town hates the idea. Everyone's going to miss you. Plus, Dallas is a big city, and you'll be by yourself." He looked at Brent. "You have to be careful. Brent can tell you."

Brent was silent for a few seconds, but Caitlin didn't miss his frown.

"He's right. You have to be careful," Brent finally said, his voice flat. Caitlin wondered again what had happened to him there. Her father wouldn't tell her a thing except that *something* had happened, and Brent had decided to return. She just didn't know what that something was. All she knew was he'd been successful working on the Dallas police force. Yet he'd still left and come home to Desmond to join a small force in a small town.

Maybe it was all part of his desire to be a dad. But anyway she looked at it, Brent wasn't for her any more than this town was. Her life awaited her, beyond the not-so-bright lights of Desmond.

"Don't start nagging, guys," Caitlin warned. "I'm moving to Dallas and that's that."

"Stupid move, squirt. You can find a good job here." Al grabbed the ball from Brent, sprinted ahead a few feet, then tossed it to Tony.

Caitlin groaned. "Living here, I hardly make enough money to buy groceries, let alone get a new car, pay rent—"

"Why not continue to live with Dad? I'm sure he'd appreciate the company now that he's all alone. . . ."

Al's words drifted off. Yeah, Dad would be alone after she left. And Caitlin, more than anyone, knew how much her father missed her mother. During the years since her mother's death, Caitlin often looked out the window of her apartment over the garage and saw her father wandering the house late at night, unable to sleep. Seeing her brother's sadness now, Caitlin walked over and gave Al a swift hug. "I know he'll be lonely, but I can't live my whole life with Dad."

Al returned her hug. "Of course not. Just until you get married."

Any kindness Caitlin had been feeling toward her younger brother shriveled up like a grape left in the sun. She pulled away from him.

"I'm not getting married, Al. Unlike you and Tony, I haven't even had a chance to start my life yet. I stayed at home first to take care of Mom and then to be with Dad. But now I need to go. This job offer is an unbelievable, once-in-a-lifetime thing. I can't pass it up."

Tony moved forward. "We all appreciated it when you put off college to take care of Mom, but—"

Tears threatened to form in Caitlin's eyes, but she forced them away. "No one has to appreciate anything. I took care of Mom because I wanted to. But now that I've graduated, it's time for me to start living my own life."

"So live here, with the rest of the family. No one's making you get married or anything," Tony argued.

"I can't live my life here. The job is in Dallas. My future is in Dallas. There are things I want to do in my life."

"What kind of things?" Tony asked.

How could her brothers be so utterly dense? Jeez. Caitlin shook her head and started to walk away. She didn't want to have this fight. Tony and Al were great brothers, and they meant well, but sometimes they just didn't get it. She'd only made it a couple of feet when Al put his hand on her arm.

"Seriously, Caitlin, why can't you just stay here?"

Exasperation boiled over, and she spun to face him. She'd had this conversation umpteen million times over the last few weeks with most of the population of Desmond. How could she possibly make them understand?

"I want the chance to prove some things to myself, and the opportunity to make a difference in this world. Good Neighbors is up and running, but I only help a handful of people. By working at the Henderson Charity, I can help hundreds, maybe even thousands. My life will matter." She sighed, then added, "Plus, all I am in this town is your sister, Dad's daughter, but never me. I need my own life."

They looked at her like she'd just fallen to earth. Mouths slightly open. Dazed looks in their eyes.

Tony recovered first. "We never meant to stop you from finding your dreams. I just always thought you liked Desmond. So what about Good Neighbors? Who will take it over when you leave?"

"That's the big question," she said, glancing quickly at Brent, then away. "I need to find someone who believes in it as much as I do."

Tony and Al looked down, as if they suddenly found their sneakers fascinating. "You know I'd take it over if I could," Al muttered. "But I'm too busy."

Before they could say much more, her brothers looked up and spotted their families arriving at their father's house. Al's wife, Madeline, and Tony's wife, Sherri, along with their daughter, Kayla, climbed out of their cars. As if thrilled with an excuse to leave, her brothers muttered good-bye and headed off at a sprint, leaving Brent and Caitlin trailing behind them.

After a few seconds, Brent asked, "What's Good Neighbors?"

Caitlin turned to face him, lifting her hair off the nape of her neck. She'd give anything for a breeze. Tilting her head, she regarded Brent, wondering how to convince him to help.

"Good Neighbors is a volunteer organization I started last year to help folks throughout the county. We do it all. Take hot meals to shut-ins, drive the elderly to their doctor appointments. You name it."

He raised one dark brow. "How do you find the time to do all that?"

The sound of his warm, husky voice distracted her. Did all women fall in love with that voice of his? So smooth, so caring. Despite the fact that he'd had a lot of girlfriends when they were growing up, Caitlin knew he'd always treated every one of them well. Most of them hadn't wanted to let him go, so finding a wife wouldn't be a problem for Brent.

Funny how that thought made her uncomfortable. But lots of things suddenly made her uncomfortable. She felt nervous, edgy around Brent. She was way too aware of him.

Pulling her gaze away from him, she studied her father's house. "Good Neighbors doesn't take up that much time. Not really. I have lots of volunteers."

"What are you going to do if you don't find someone to take your place?"

The thought of Good Neighbors dissolving made

Caitlin's throat tighten with pain, but she had to stand firm. She couldn't let this job at Henderson pass her by. She'd only gotten it in the first place because of the great article the Dallas paper had run about Good Neighbors. She'd never get another opportunity like it. So whether she found a replacement here in Desmond or not, she had to leave at the end of the month.

It was as simple as that.

"I'm moving even if I don't find someone to take over Good Neighbors," Caitlin said. "I know it may sound strange, but by moving to Dallas, I can end up helping so many more people than if I'm stuck here in Desmond."

"But won't they just be different people you're helping?"

Caitlin looked at him without immediately replying. She checked both directions, then headed across the street, leading the way to her father's house.

"I guess it's hard for everyone in town to understand," Caitlin said.

"Maybe that's because most people don't think Dallas is the right place for you."

Oh, great. Just great. Now he was going to join the crowd that wanted to change her mind about the move. But she wanted this chance. The job was terrific. Her future looked bright. She was going to fulfill her dreams.

"The decision isn't up to those people. Besides, I won't know that until I try," she said, heading across the front lawn.

Brent stopped her by putting his hand on her arm. "A bigger town doesn't make life simpler. In fact, when I first got to Dallas, I was damn lonely. And then—"

When tingles danced up her arm at his touch, she pulled free of his grasp. "And then you probably met someone wonderful, and eventually you weren't lonely anymore, right? You did exciting things with fascinating people. People you hadn't gone to school with, people who didn't know every tiny embarrassing thing you'd done in your life. No, you got to try new things and meet new people. I want that, too, and best of all, at the same time I'll be able to do a meaningful job that makes a difference in this world."

Brent stared at her as if she were a cat who had suddenly started to speak. "Are you really that unhappy here?"

"It's not so much that I'm unhappy; I just feel . . . contained."

"Maybe if you got a new boyfriend. Maybe that would spice up your life. Your brothers told me you aren't seeing anyone."

His comment surprised her, mostly because she couldn't help wondering if he'd asked for that information or if Tony or Al had volunteered it. But either way, it didn't matter.

"I don't need a boyfriend, Brent. What everyone doesn't understand is I'm not running away from Desmond; I'm going to Dallas. There's a difference." Her voice trailed off as she stared up at him.

Brent moved forward, placing both hands on her arms this time and turning her to face him.

"Honey, then you should do what you need to do." He glanced at her father's house, and then looked back at her. "You should follow your dreams."

Hope grew inside Caitlin. Since he felt that way,

maybe he would help. She looked him straight in the eye and went for broke.

"Then be my buddy, Brent, and help me. Make it possible for me to leave Desmond. Make it possible for me to have my dreams. Take over Good Neighbors."

Chapter Two

Brent stood on the patio of Dan Rogers's house, still debating Caitlin's request. Truthfully, he didn't know what to tell her. Sure, he'd like to help, but he'd just moved back to town, just started his new job. He didn't have a lot of time, and more than likely, running something like this Good Neighbors program was a huge undertaking.

He couldn't help wishing he'd get a chance to talk to Caitlin. He had lots of questions, but so far, he hadn't had the opportunity to ask them. After she'd made her request, she'd hurriedly told him to take his time thinking about it. Then she'd sprinted into the house—and proceeded to avoid him. Dan Rogers had invited him to stay for dinner, but now Brent questioned the wisdom of accepting. All evening, Caitlin had ducked and dodged him, making certain her family surrounded her.

She obviously was afraid he'd turn her down. Of course, there was more to it than that. The attraction between them was unnerving. He felt it, too. After dinner, hoping for some time to think, he'd volunteered to go outside and clean the barbecue grill. Truthfully, he'd wanted to consider not only his answer but also his questions. He didn't want to sound like a heartless jerk when he talked this over with Caitlin. Saying no sounded selfish, but saying yes sounded like a lot of work.

From inside the house, he could vaguely hear the laughter and conversation of the Rogers family—people who treated him like he was part of their family, too. That was the problem. How could he turn Caitlin Rogers down?

Glancing next door, he looked at his house. Before he'd come to live there, he'd never had a home. Then, when he'd been ten, his mother had dropped him off so he could visit his grandmother for the summer. She'd never come back to get him. With a quick kiss, she'd left him there, and poof! She was no longer a mom. Just like that.

He would have been miserable if it hadn't been for the Rogers family. Tony and Al had befriended him, making sure he met everyone in Desmond. And more than once, Dan Rogers had convinced his grandmother to lighten up on him. Afraid he'd turn out as flighty as his mother, his grandmother had made him toe the line. But Dan had saved him. Since he was the police chief, Marie Stewart had listened to Dan.

And then there was Alexis Rogers. His grandmother had also listened to Alexis, a gentle woman who always had a ready smile or hug for her children and the boy next door. Alexis had been a great lady, and Brent still missed her.

When he heard the back door to the house open, he didn't bother turning around. Heavy footsteps signaled Dan approaching.

"You missed a spot," Dan said, coming to stand next to him.

Brent glanced down at the still filthy barbecue rack in his hands. "Looks to me like I've missed quite a few spots."

Dan chuckled. "True." For several moments, he was silent, so Brent went back to work. He'd learned a long time ago that Dan spoke in his own time, at his own pace. He was a man who carefully considered his words, which was probably what made him such a great police chief. He never rushed to judgment, never spoke in haste.

After the silence grew uncomfortable, Brent said, "Nice night."

"Sure is, if you like air hotter than the devil's butt and filled with enough bugs to choke a frog." Dan scratched his chin. "But that's not what I came out here for. I want to ask you something."

Brent stopped scrubbing and looked at Dan. For some unexplained reason, he tensed, bracing himself for what the older man had to say. "What?"

"I was wondering if Caitlin asked you to take over her Good Neighbors program."

"She asked, but I haven't given her an answer yet," Brent admitted. "I'm not sure what I'd be committing to if I said yes."

Dan nodded his head. "Smart move. It's a lot of work, but you'd have help. Most folks in town are pitching in whenever and wherever it's needed. Just last week, I brought meals to Lois Phillips while she recovered from her appendectomy.''

Brent already knew he wanted to help in some way. It was the thought of actually running the organization that made him hesitate. At the moment, though, he was trying to figure out if Dan was encouraging or discouraging him from saying yes. "I don't know if I'll have enough time to run it.''

"Is that your only concern?" Dan asked.

Brent turned and studied Dan. As his boss, Dan had to have an opinion about him taking on Good Neighbors. But whatever it was, Dan was keeping it to himself.

"Pretty much. I've only been back a little over a week. I don't really have my bearings yet.''

"I bet," Dan said. "But I was curious 'cause I thought you might be like the rest of us. We're hoping Caitlin will change her mind about this move. It's going to leave a big hole in Desmond when she's gone.''

That comment got Brent's attention. Apparently, no one was thrilled about Caitlin's decision. That had to make it difficult on her. He knew how much she loved her family, but just from their brief conversation this afternoon, he knew how much her new job meant to her, too.

"But don't you think she has the right to do some of the things she wants to do in life?" Brent pointed out.

Before Dan could respond, the back door opened again. This time, Brent knew immediately it was Caitlin. The sweet, sexy scent she wore teased him long before she spoke.

"Are you two hiding out here?" Her tentative smile didn't quite reach her eyes.

Dan moved across the patio and draped his arm around her shoulders. "I just came out to chat with Brent."

Caitlin looked from her father to Brent, then back at her father. "Really? You're not the 'chatting' type, Dad."

Dan patted her shoulder. "Maybe I've changed. Maybe now I like to chat."

Caitlin laughed. "Oh, right, I believe that."

With a chuckle, Dan said, "Either way, I think I'll go yell at your brothers just for old times' sake." With a grin, he headed back inside.

Brent half expected Caitlin to follow Dan, but she didn't. Instead, she stayed out with him, shutting the door behind her father. Nodding toward the grill, she said, "You know, you don't have to clean that."

Although she was facing him, she wasn't making eye contact. Brent hated how awkward they were around each other, but he hadn't a clue how to change things. He couldn't just turn off the attraction he felt for her.

"Cleaning the grill is the least I can do since your family fed me," he said.

Caitlin dropped into one of the lawn chairs on the porch and studied him. "We feed a lot of people, and they don't clean the grill."

"They should." She raised one eyebrow, but said nothing. Finally, he shrugged. "I always help clean up. You know that."

"You're an exceptionally responsible person, Brent."

After a moment's hesitation, her gaze met and held his. Brent felt the question hovering between them, but he also felt the unmistakable sizzle of sexual awareness. That awareness added an entirely new wrinkle to this problem. If he did agree to take over Good Neighbors, wouldn't they have to spend a lot of time together over the next month to get him up to speed? What if something happened and they acted on the attraction between them? They could both end up getting hurt.

At this moment, the tension between them crackled, and he knew Caitlin felt it as much as he did. He couldn't deny even to himself that he desired her, and it was clear that she was interested.

Well, hell.

Acting on the attraction between them would be stupid. No, beyond stupid. Idiotic. Caitlin had plans in Dallas, and he wanted—no, needed—to settle down here. There was no future for them, and he didn't want to settle for anything less.

She sat looking at him expectantly, so finally he said, "You're a responsible person, too."

Caitlin laughed softly and glanced away, breaking the dangerous connection between them. "Ah, gee, we're both just swell, aren't we?"

Brent smiled. "A couple of great guys . . . er, people."

"So have you had a chance to think about Good Neighbors yet? I'll understand if you say no. But you would be great at it. Exactly what I need." Her soft voice drifted across the still night air, wrapping seductively around him, tempting him to agree.

But he couldn't just say yes. He wasn't that befuddled. He needed to understand the commitment before he could make it. "Even though we're friends, I'm not sure I can say yes or no until I understand what running Good Neighbors would involve. I have a full-time job. Could I work around my shifts? What exactly would I be promising?"

"Those are fair questions," she said. "I could show you what I do, take you around and let you meet some of the other volunteers and then maybe some of the people who need Good Neighbors' services."

Brent could tell from the trace of excitement in her voice that she thought he was going to agree. She might be right. There was a fairly good chance he would agree, but not until he had a better handle on this.

"I'm not promising anything, Caitlin," he warned her.

She nodded, her dark hair moving sensuously against her neck. "I understand, and I'm not trying to pressure you. Just because we're buddies doesn't mean you owe me anything."

Brent frowned. Lots of things about that statement bothered him. First, they weren't buddies. Not anymore. He wouldn't feel like this about a buddy. Second, if anyone had kept score while they were growing up, he probably did owe Caitlin. She had helped him out of quite a few jams when they'd been kids.

But he didn't say anything, so Caitlin continued, her voice becoming softer, more thoughtful. "It's important that someone reliable takes over after I leave."

"Why? If no one wants to take over, then the organization can just dissolve."

Caitlin reacted like he'd hit her in the face with a fish. "I would hate it if that happened," she said. "Everyone has worked so hard, even though I truthfully never thought Good Neighbors would turn into much."

"What made you start it in the first place?"

She seemed almost self-conscious as she explained, "Well, Dad was always telling me about calls y'all get at the station, calls that aren't a police emergency, just someone in need. I know a few of the churches try to help out, but a lot of folks still slip through the cracks. If we lived in a big city, there would be all sorts of programs to help out. But since we're too tiny for any of the big charities, I thought . . ." She shrugged. "I thought I'd see if I could help."

Caitlin had always been, and obviously still was, a big softie at heart. She brought home strays. Animals, people. Anyone who needed anything had always gone to Caitlin. He sure had. More than once, he'd gone to her to make him feel better after breaking up with a girlfriend. She'd challenge him to a game of basketball, during which he'd whine about the treachery of Cindy or Denise or Jennifer. By the end of the game, he'd feel much better. That was the kind of person Caitlin was. She made people feel better.

Looking at her now, knowing how sweet she was, seeing how sexy she was, he wondered why he hadn't fallen for her years ago. Maybe he really was stupid.

"Have you made a difference around town?" he asked.

This time when she smiled, her pretty eyes lit with humor. "I hope so. I never expected as many people to volunteer as have. Everyone's been great." She arched one brow. "I also greatly underestimated the number of requests for help we'd get."

"Won't you miss Good Neighbors?" He finished

cleaning the rack and rinsed it off. "Seems to me it would be difficult to walk away from something you'd put so much time into."

"Yes, I'll miss it. But my new job will be a chance to do a lot more, help thousands of people."

"Not to mention the chance to live someplace you find more exciting than Desmond." Brent turned his head to look at her. Their gazes met and held in the pale twilight.

Caitlin laughed softly and looked at her hands in her lap. "Oh, so now I know what Dad came out to talk to you about. I can hear him now. 'Why is Caitlin leaving? Doesn't she know how much everyone in town needs her?' " She blew out a loud sigh. "I know everyone wants me to stay, but I just can't. I can't pass up this job, and the truth is, I don't want to pass it up." She tipped her head, her blue eyes meeting his again. "Why is that so wrong? You wanted to work in Dallas, so you did. No one tried to make you feel guilty. Why shouldn't I have the same chance?"

Her intense gaze did funny things to him, but he refused to think about his reaction right now. Focusing on the grill, he reassembled it and put the cover on. Satisfied he'd done a good job, he washed his hands with water from the hose and the soap he'd used on the grill. Finally, when he had no other reason to avoid her, he came over and sat in the chair next to hers. Why did she have to be so pretty? Why couldn't she still be the kid he'd grown up with? Then agreeing to work with her would be easy.

But she wasn't a kid anymore. She'd turned into a beautiful woman, and probably partially as a result of losing her mother, she'd matured. Gone was the Caitlin he remembered, the young girl always laughing, always joking. This Caitlin was new to him. She still smiled, but when she did, it was a woman's smile. One with the power to make him stop and notice.

And think a few thoughts he ought not be thinking. Focusing back on what she'd said, he studied her. "You're preaching to the choir, Caitlin. Like I said before, I think you should be able to follow your dreams. But I'm not sure I'm the right person to take over."

His comment earned him an unladylike groan. "Oh, please, you're terrific and you know it."

Terrific? She thought he was terrific? "Maybe I'm not anymore. You're remembering what I was like as a kid. Maybe I'm a terrible person now."

She leaned forward and tapped his arm lightly. "People don't change that much, not really. They don't change what they're like deep down. You were always the first one to help out when we were kids."

Brent laughed. "No. You were always the first one to help out when we were kids. I was dragged along by you like everyone else."

"You're a great guy, and you know it. We wouldn't be friends if you weren't."

Deep down, he wasn't sure how to respond to that statement or the sweet way she said it. He wasn't feeling like such a great guy at the moment. A great guy would have agreed without hesitation. And a great guy wouldn't be sitting here thinking lustful thoughts about a woman who'd always been one of his best friends.

"Did you ask me because there isn't anyone else to ask?"

She groaned. "No, and don't be a doofus. There are lots of people I can ask, but I haven't. I want the person who takes over Good Neighbors to be someone special, someone perfect for the job."

He chuckled, but it made him feel strange when she referred to him as perfect. "You can't seriously think I'm perfect."

She gave him a don't-be-a-dope look. "You're perfect for this job."

Damn, but he didn't like being in this position, standing between Caitlin and her dreams. Before he could say anything else, she leaned toward him and said, "Brent, I've spent the past four years waiting for something like this. Suddenly, because of the newspaper article about Good Neighbors, this exciting job just dropped into my lap. Kapow! Don't get me wrong; I'm glad I put off starting my career while I stayed here and took care of Mom. But I also saw what happened to her dreams. She died without doing half the things she wanted to do. I don't want that to happen to me."

"And you can't have your dreams if you stay here?"

"The only dream I could fulfill in Desmond is to get married and have children. But that's not what I want. I don't want to stay home and play wifey to some good ol' boy."

This conversation made him uncomfortable, probably because he did want to settle down in Desmond. Still, he felt he had to point out, "You might not hate being married if you met the right guy."

She shook her head emphatically. "No. I won't give up my dreams for anyone. Not even for a man who"—she shrugged—"floats my boat."

Brent laughed, glad to feel the tension between

them break. "Sure about that? Not even if he scaled your wall?"

"Or bagged my lunch?"

"Or browned your toast?"

Caitlin was laughing in earnest now, and she put her hand on his arm. "Stop it."

Brent grinned at her. He'd always liked being around Caitlin. And as he'd discovered today, he was attracted to her, too. Attracted enough that he didn't like thinking about Caitlin's love life. Which was bizarre since he'd never been overprotective of her. He left that job up to Tony and Al. She wasn't his sister, and he'd never felt brotherly toward her. And he sure as hell didn't feel brotherly toward her now.

His gaze dropped to her full lips, which were slightly moist and parted. Suddenly, it felt unbearably hot out here on the porch, and Brent would have suggested moving inside to join the rest of her family if he didn't know how much it meant to her to resolve this now.

"What happens if I say no?"

She turned in her chair to face him. "I'm still going to Dallas." Caitlin gave him a look that heated the blood in his veins. "Is it really so much to ask that you be a hero and help me out?"

No, it wasn't. And with sudden clarity, he knew why he wasn't agreeing to help. He hated to admit it, even to himself, but he *was* like everyone else in Desmond. He didn't want Caitlin to leave, especially now when he'd discovered that she . . . well, floated his boat.

"Give me a day or so to think about it," he finally said, knowing he'd disappointed her but needing more time.

* * *

"How's the birthday girl?" her father asked the following evening when Caitlin came through the side door a few minutes before her party was to start.

"I'm great. And excited." When she reached his side, Caitlin stood on tiptoe and kissed her dad on the cheek. She loved him and always had. Dan Rogers had heaped praise on his children, delighting in their accomplishments, and he'd never once tried to force them into his way of thinking. Well, almost never. And as much as Caitlin was looking forward to getting her own place and starting her own life, she would miss her dad.

"You look great." He took her hand and spun her lightly, whistling at her dress. "I'm going to have to keep a close watch on the boys and make certain they don't get any ideas."

Caitlin smiled and glanced around, hoping Brent might have arrived already. Surely by now he'd have made a decision. Unfortunately, she had the gut feeling he was going to say no.

If he did, she'd be back to square one. She didn't want to leave without a replacement, but if she had to, she would. Well, if Brent did turn her down, at least most of the town would be here tonight. Maybe she could find someone else to ask. She could only hope it wouldn't come to that. She'd keep her fingers crossed that Brent would come through for her.

Turning, she surveyed the room. Her brothers and their wives, Madeline and Sherri, had outdone themselves. White and silver crepe paper crisscrossed the entryway to each room, while balloons seemed to be everywhere. But the banister was her favorite part.

Tiny white twinkle lights twined up the oak rails, giving the house a fairyland feel. She knew her brothers and Brent had spent most of last night stringing similar lights out back and setting up a dance floor in the center of the yard. Off to the side, they'd built a small stage for the local bands to perform on. No doubt about it, her birthday party was going to be a major event for the town of Desmond.

Madeline came out of the kitchen, carrying bowls of snacks. When she saw Caitlin, she grinned. "Wow, you look gorgeous." She set the bowls on the dining room table and patted her large belly. "Here I am, not sure my shoes match, and you look hot—" She glanced at her father-in-law, then with a sheepish grin, backpedaled. "I mean, you look lovely."

Caitlin returned her sister-in-law's smile. She liked both of the women her brothers had married. Sherri was quieter than Madeline, but they were both genuinely nice people.

"Anything I can do to help?" Caitlin asked. She went to stand next to Madeline, barely resisting the urge to pat the other woman's stomach. Funny how the sight of a pregnant woman made people do the oddest things.

"Nope. Sherri and I have your brothers doing KP duty, so we're all set." She looked over at Dan. "Dad, I think you'd better reserve the first dance with Caitlin here. The guys are going to be all over her like bees on a flower. Maybe one of them will sweep her off her feet and get her to rethink Dallas."

Her dad grinned at her. "I'd love it if Caity would stay put. She's a sweet lady, just like her mother was, and some man's going to be darn lucky to have her. All she needs to do is find the right guy."

As he was speaking, Caitlin resisted the impulse to groan. Her father would never figure her out no matter how old she got. As he went on listing all of the qualities he thought she possessed that would make her a good wife, Caitlin heard the front door open. When the sound of laughter and kidding reached her, she knew without even looking that Brent had arrived. Just in time to hear her father's words. She glanced over her shoulder, praying she was wrong. But sure enough, he stood in the doorway, watching her.

Even though the party was casual, he wore perfectly pressed khaki twill pants and an off-white banded-collar shirt. Brent had always been a great dresser. Most guys she knew would just pull on a pair of clean jeans and a T-shirt. But not Brent. He looked like something off the pages of *GQ*. Tall. Handsome. Sexy.

Hot.

Holy cow. Brent looked good enough to tempt a saint. Forcing those thoughts to the back of her mind, Caitlin gave him a tentative smile, hoping to sense his mood. She'd dropped off a lot of information about Good Neighbors at his house earlier. Had he read it? Made a decision? She couldn't tell anything from his expression, not even when he returned her smile.

"Happy birthday, Caitlin," he said, moving into the room.

"Thank you." Before she could say anything else, he handed her a small, rectangular box wrapped in pretty gold paper.

Madeline stepped forward, eyeing the box. "Ooh. Boxes that look like that usually have the very best presents inside." Her sister-in-law took the present from her and set it on the sideboard with the other gifts.

Caitlin glanced briefly at Madeline and then looked again at Brent. She saw good, old-fashioned male interest in his gaze. He hadn't told her she looked pretty, but she could tell from the way he looked at her that he thought she was. Was that part of the reason he wasn't agreeing? Was he upset about this newly discovered attraction between them?

"Thank you for the present, Brent," she said softly.

Brent smiled. "I hope you like it."

The doorbell rang then, and a flood of people entered, moving forward to congratulate her. For the next half hour, Caitlin only caught brief glimpses of Brent as he moved through the crowd. She desperately wanted to talk to him, but she could hardly do that since it seemed as if every square inch of her father's house was filled with family and friends.

Just when she thought she'd explode with tension, her father appeared by her side and took her hand. "I think this is my dance. Come on, let's head outside."

Caitlin smiled at him, excused herself from the people she'd been talking with, and then followed him as he wove through the crowd. When they reached the back porch, she stopped, staring with amazement at the backyard.

"It's so beautiful," she murmured, moving forward. White lights twinkled from the trees, from the fence, from the small stage. Tears welled up in Caitlin's eyes. Her family was so sweet. They could have just bought her a cake and wished her a happy birthday. Instead, they'd pulled out all the stops, making her last birthday spent at home something really special.

Her father took her hand and led her to the dance floor. As the band launched into a slow waltz, Caitlin knew something significant was happening here. Something more meaningful than simply getting a year older. She was late starting her life, late getting out on her own. Suddenly, she realized what this moment meant. It was a rite of passage. Next time she danced with her father, she'd be a career woman on her own, an independent person making her way in the world. She wouldn't simply be Dan Rogers's little girl anymore.

As much as the idea thrilled her, a little twinge of regret flittered through her. She tightened the hand her father held, holding on to him. Although she didn't want to make him cry, she leaned forward and through her tear-tightened throat whispered, "Mom would have loved this."

Rather than being sad, her dad twirled her and chuckled. "You bet. She loved a fuss, and you don't get a bigger fuss than this." Turning serious, he smiled down at her. "She'd be proud of you, Caitlin."

Caitlin nodded, unable to get words out. Yes, her mother had wanted her to be happy, to follow her dreams. For years, she'd tried to convince Caitlin to move out, to start her own life, to stop worrying about her. But Caitlin couldn't. She'd wanted every single day she could have with her mother, and she'd never regretted for a moment postponing her own plans. Just like she didn't regret living at home until her father had a chance to get used to her mother being gone.

When the song ended, Caitlin kissed her father's sun-weathered cheek. "I love you, Dad."

He grinned down at her. "I love you, too, sweetie."

Glancing over his shoulder, he added, "I think the crowd of young men is about to steal you away from me."

Then with a hug, he walked away. Caitlin started to follow him when her brother Al grabbed her and swung her in the air.

"Come on, let's really dance." With that, he hollered at the band, which launched into a loud rendition of a rock and roll favorite.

"Don't let them get too loud," Caitlin said to Al, trying to be heard over the music. Al seemed unconcerned about the volume. Instead, he did a series of gyrations that had Caitlin laughing. "What are you doing?"

"Don't I remind you of John Travolta disco dancing?"

"No. You remind me of a man with his finger in a light socket."

With a laugh, Al continued to bop and hop until the song ended. Then he gave Caitlin a loud kiss on her cheek. "See ya, kid. I've got to go find that lovely, pregnant lady who's been lusting after me all night."

As Al sprinted off, the band started a slow love song, so Caitlin headed toward the house. But before she took three steps, a large, tanned hand touched her arm.

"Dance with me, Caitlin."

She drew a shallow breath into her suddenly tight chest. Forcing what she hoped was a natural smile onto her face, she turned toward Brent. Being this close to him, looking up into his handsome face, was disconcerting. Her pulse picked up, and for a moment, she just stared at him. He was so gorgeous.

"Sure," she said, amazed at the steadiness of her

voice, telling herself silently to stay calm. After all, it wouldn't be the end of the world if he said no. Just a setback. But as much as she tried to keep her mind on the question at hand, she couldn't help focusing instead on the sensations flooding through her body as they started to dance. She could think of no other place on earth she'd rather be than in the arms of this man.

Chapter Three

Stepping into Brent's open embrace, Caitlin held her breath as he pulled her close. He had to feel the slight tremble that ran through her at his touch, had to know how he affected her. She couldn't help wondering what he thought about this attraction between them.

Aware of the other couples around them on the makeshift dance floor, Caitlin avoided asking the question she was dying to ask. Instead, she concentrated on the pleasure of being held by such a handsome man. He clasped one of her hands tightly in his own, their fingers intertwined. Her other hand rested on his shoulder. Without meaning to, she flexed her fingers and then lightly rubbed his shirt. The texture of the oxford cloth tickled her fingertips. She couldn't tell if it was the result of her caress or not, but Brent slipped the hand on her back lower until it rested on her waist. She could feel each of his fingers through the thin material of her dress. And when his thighs brushed hers, she leaned into him. Her breasts felt heavy, swollen. Her breathing grew shallow.

Holy cow. Talk about dangerous. She couldn't get distracted by Brent now. Not now when so much depended on keeping her focus.

"I'll do it."

She had been so caught up in the sensations he was creating in her body that it took a second for his softly spoken words to sink in. When they did, joy rushed through her. All right. He'd said yes. She'd been prepared for a no. Heck, she'd already written down the names of other possible candidates. But Brent had come through for her. Now she could leave Desmond with no regrets.

"You are the best," she said, meaning it. "The absolute best buddy in the world." She knew Brent hadn't agreed for any reason other than he was her friend. Her own brothers had been unwilling to help her, but Brent had said yes.

He shifted until his gaze caught and held hers. Then, he lightly touched her face. "You're a pretty good buddy, too."

His words were innocent, but there was nothing innocent in his touch or the husky tone of his voice. Trying to douse the fire building between them, she smiled and said, "This means so much to me, Brent. Really. You've given me a future."

Brent stopped dancing. "You really don't feel like you can have a future unless you leave Desmond, do you?"

"No, I don't."

Apparently aware once more of the other couples around them, Brent started dancing again. "You know, I moved back to Desmond because I missed the place. And here everyone in town thinks you're the best thing to come along since chocolate candy, and you can't wait to leave."

"Funny how it's worked out, isn't it?"

Brent shifted her a tiny bit closer in his arms. "It's just hard to believe we both grew up in this town, yet see it so differently."

She sighed, relaxing in his embrace. "Maybe that's because you had the chance to live someplace else, to have new experiences."

"But in my case, those experiences convinced me I'd made a mistake leaving Desmond. You might find that you miss everyone once you've left."

The last notes of the song came to an end, and Brent stopped dancing. For a timeless moment, they just looked at each other.

"Happy birthday," he said, then leaned down and brushed his firm lips lightly against her own. The kiss was soft, but when he lingered, a jolt ran through her.

When Brent finally lifted his head, he looked directly into her eyes. "For the record, I'm going to miss you, Caitlin," he said, his deep voice husky.

"Um, I'll miss you, too." Holy, *holy* cow. Brent had kissed her. Wow.

With one final squeeze, he let go of her hand and removed his other hand from her back. Despite the warm temperature of the night air, Caitlin felt chilled.

"Thanks for the dance, and thanks again for agreeing to help," she said, the kiss still lingering in her mind and on her lips.

Brent nodded, then said, "I'll do my best. But to be honest, I'm just like everyone else around here. If I knew how to do it, I'd probably try to change your mind."

On Monday, Brent sat in his patrol car, watching for speeders and still annoyed at himself for telling Caitlin he'd try to change her mind about leaving. What right did he have to say that to her? She deserved the chance to follow her dreams. What good did it do to make her feel guilty?

And he had made her feel guilty. At least a little. He could tell from the way the shine had dimmed in her eyes. Hell, he hadn't meant to do that. It was like stomping on a child's sand castle. But deep down, he hated the thought of her moving to Dallas, a place where no one would give a damn about her.

He knew he was being silly. Caitlin would make friends; she always did. People loved Caitlin. A new, and unnerving thought zipped through his mind. She'd probably find some guy in Dallas, too. Maybe even eventually get married.

Which made him feel . . . weird. Kissing her on Saturday had been flat-out stupid, especially after the attraction that had sizzled between them the last few days. His only excuse was he hadn't been able to stop himself. At the party, she'd looked so beautiful in that silky sundress of hers. When he'd held her close, his hand on her back, he'd realized she hadn't been wearing a bra under it. Her generous breasts had pressed against his chest, and he'd had to shift her more than once so she wouldn't feel how aroused he'd gotten simply by touching her. Holding her. Wanting her.

He vividly remembered her look when she'd opened his present later that night. She'd gasped at the sight of the simple gold chain and heart locket, making him glad he'd chosen it for her. When she'd looked at him from across the room, he'd seen the genuine surprise and pleasure in her gaze. Madeline had fastened the necklace around Caitlin's neck. Then Caitlin had lifted the heart. Without shifting her gaze from his, she'd slipped the heart under the fabric of her dress, sliding it into the valley between her breasts. A faint sweat had broken out on his forehead as he'd held her gaze. He'd wanted her then. Badly.

Then she'd laughed at something someone else had said, and the spell had been broken. But even now, he still wanted her . . . He just wasn't going to do anything about it. Okay, sure, he was attracted to Caitlin. *Really* attracted to her. But dammit, he wanted to settle down, and Caitlin had no intention of changing her plans. So sex between them would be wrong.

A red Corvette roared by him, and Brent pulled his attention back to his job. He didn't need his radar gun to tell him he had a speeder, but he still clocked the driver. Then he started his car and headed off. Whoever was out to break the sound barrier wasn't from around here, or they would have known better. And they were about to pay the price for breaking the speed limit in Desmond, Texas.

Caitlin squinted at the computer screen in the Desmond library, trying to find a book Mabel Dawson would like. Boy, did this place need some new equipment. Maybe there was some way Good Neighbors could help. They could hold a fund-raiser to buy new computers. But she wouldn't be the one to do that. She'd have to mention it to Brent and see if he wanted to look into it.

The thought of walking away from Good Neighbors sure felt strange. She'd devoted so much time and energy to it over the last few months that it was almost always on her mind. It would take her a while to let go.

Of course, even a state-of-the-art computer system wouldn't help in her current quest. This afternoon, she and Brent were taking a hot meal over to Mrs. Mabel Dawson, a lifelong town resident approaching her nineties. Mabel had asked if they would also bring her a few books on Europe from the library. It seemed the sweet lady had recently decided that somehow, some way, her family was related to European royalty. She didn't have a preference for any particular country, just an absolutely unshakeable belief that blue blood flowed in her veins.

Caitlin jotted down the names of the few books the library had that might interest Mabel. Glancing at her watch, she saw she still had quite a while before Brent was due to meet her here. In a way, she wasn't looking forward to an afternoon with him, even if it would be spent making calls for Good Neighbors. No way could they pretend things were still normal between them. Not after he'd kissed her.

Well, they'd just have to put the whole thing behind them. They had too much to do over the next few weeks to obsess over one silly kiss. It had been her birthday, after all. The kiss had probably meant nothing. At least, it had probably meant nothing to Brent.

She, on the other hand, could almost still feel it, still taste it. It had practically curled her toes.

But she needed to put that blasted kiss out of her mind. She had other things to think about. Heading down the aisle, she picked up a couple of books people had left on the floor and tucked them under her arm. Then she grabbed two books on French history for Mabel, and returned to the front of the library.

On the way, she studied the stray books she'd found. One was a book on etiquette written almost twenty years ago. The other book was a how-to manual, *Creating A New You,* written by a supermodel the year before last. Caitlin decided to check out the how-to book herself. Wasn't that what she was about to do? Create a new Caitlin?

Idly, she fingered the gold chain around her neck, enjoying the feel of the gold locket resting between her breasts. Seemed no matter how hard she tried, she kept thinking about Brent. His gift on Saturday had stunned her. It was so pretty, so personal. He'd had the locket engraved with her name, showing he'd given her birthday some thought.

Yep, the man definitely fell into the great guy category. She smiled thinking about how sexy Brent had looked Saturday night. Not only was he a great guy, he was great looking, too. She'd have to watch herself. She didn't want to do something foolish like fall for him. The last thing she needed to take with her to Dallas was a broken heart.

After checking out the books and chatting with the librarian, Vanda Capilli, for a few minutes, Caitlin looked around for an empty table. She still had a lot of time to kill before Brent was due to meet her. The library was fairly crowded, but she eventually found an unoccupied table off by itself near the back. Brent would just have to look for her.

Curious, she flipped through the pages of the supermodel's book. There were hints about makeup and clothes and hairstyles. But Chapter fourteen was the one that really caught her attention. It described ways to attract a man. Caitlin settled back in her chair and started to read, a smile teasing her lips. Maybe if she did the exact opposite of everything it said in this book she might find a way to "unattract" Brent. Heck, anything was worth a try.

"Nice little town you've got here," said the driver of the Corvette, a flashy blond guy from Dallas named Mason Gibbs.

Brent handed the man his ticket and returned his license and registration. He didn't like this guy, and not just because he'd been unrepentant when pulled over. Gibbs acted like the whole thing was a joke. It riled Brent, but he made certain to keep his attitude in check.

"Those of us who live here like Desmond a lot. And we want to keep the town safe, so mind the speed limit."

The man nodded. "Oh, yeah. Sure thing." He tucked his license back into a wallet even Brent could tell was expensive. "Mind telling me where Juniper Street is? My aunt lives there."

Since Brent knew almost everyone who lived in town, undoubtedly he could help with more than just directions to the street. "What's her name?"

"Vanda Capilli."

It figured this guy was related to Vanda. The older

woman was full of juice and had been pulled over more times than he could count. But whether he liked this guy or not, it was Brent's job to be polite, so he gave the man directions. "I know Vanda. Head east until you come to Turner Lane. Take a left. Juniper is the second street on the right. And Vanda's house is midway down the first block. A white two-story with green trim. But you probably won't find her there right now. Vanda works at the library. It's on Turner Lane. You'll see it right after you turn."

"Thanks. I'll stop by there first." Mason Gibbs grinned at Brent. "See ya, Officer." With that, he pulled his Corvette back into traffic.

Brent muttered a well-chosen curse and headed back to his patrol car. He didn't need to deal with this jerkface today. Thankfully, Desmond was far enough away from most interstates and they didn't get a lot of the folks just driving through. Like Mason Gibbs, most new people in town were moving to Desmond or visiting family.

But he knew Gibbs bothered him a lot more than he should. Brent also knew why. Because that guy was the type waiting for someone sweet like Caitlin. A smooth, good-looking snake who'd take advantage of her in a heartbeat. Dallas was crawling with guys just like him.

Dammit. The library. He'd just sent that jerk to the library. The library where he was meeting Caitlin after his shift ended. Brent glanced at his watch. Maybe she wouldn't show up until after Mason Gibbs had left. Maybe that sleaze wouldn't meet her. Maybe for once life would work out the way it should rather than the way it always did.

Yeah, right. And maybe he'd become the next quarterback for the Dallas Cowboys.

Brent groaned. He had to stop thinking about Caitlin this way. She was leaving. He was staying. Sure, they had this incredible chemistry going on right now, but it wasn't going to lead anywhere. What did he care if Gibbs bumped into Caitlin and asked her out? She was a big girl who could handle herself.

As much as Brent hated to admit it, even though he didn't want to get involved with Caitlin, he also didn't like the idea of her getting involved with someone else. Talk about stupid. He was so confused about Caitlin, he'd obviously lost his mind.

"I'm as big a jerkface as Gibbs," he muttered, staring out into the hot Texas sun.

"Excuse me."

Caitlin jumped a tiny bit, startled. Feeling guilty, she slammed the supermodel's book shut and looked up at the man standing next to the table. Wow. He was really good-looking, but she couldn't help thinking he wasn't nearly as good-looking as Brent. Well, maybe it was just because this man was so different from Brent. While they were both tall, this man had blond hair and pale blue eyes. He wore his hair long, well over his collar, and he had a diamond stud in his left earlobe. He flashed her a grin, and Caitlin couldn't help smiling back.

"Yes?" she asked.

The man leaned forward and she caught a whiff of his cologne. Patiently, she waited for the scent to affect her the way Brent's cologne did, but oddly enough, nothing happened.

"First things first. My name's Mason Gibbs. I'm Vanda Capilli's nephew." He extended his hand. "You're Caitlin Rogers, right?"

"Yes." She shook his hand and wasn't a bit surprised when he didn't release her hand immediately. He held it noticeably too long, his gaze never wavering from her face. Covertly she checked his left hand and saw no wedding ring. Of course, that didn't mean anything, but it didn't hurt.

Finally, Mason let go of her hand, then rested against the table, glancing down at the book she'd been reading. "Caitlin, why would you want to read her book? You don't need any help." His cool gaze returned to her face. "You're so pretty."

Smooth. Although she was flattered by this man's compliments, her heart wasn't slamming in her chest the way it did when she talked with Brent. Still, Mason Gibbs was attractive and seemed very nice, and she did need to stop thinking about Brent.

"Thank you," she said, at a loss as to the proper response. "Is there something you want?"

The man quirked one blond brow, and at first she was afraid he'd tease her about her innocent question. But he let it slide.

"My aunt asked me to bring you this," he said.

Only then did Caitlin realize he held a book in one hand. Tipping her head, she saw the book was on English royalty. Mason gave it to Caitlin, then recited, "Aunt Vanda said to tell you that Mabel might like this one." He grinned. "Does that message make sense to you?"

Caitlin returned his smile. "Yes. Thank you."

"My pleasure. Now maybe you can do something for me. I'm stuck here waiting for my aunt to get off work, and I'm hoping this library has some newspapers to read. Can you save me from abject boredom and show me where they are?''

He said the last sentence so melodramatically that Caitlin laughed and stood. ''Follow me. They don't have a huge selection, but I think you'll find something you like.''

As she led the way to where the newspapers and magazines were, she got the distinct feeling Mason Gibbs was checking her out. Guys had checked her out before, but not for a while. In high school and her first couple of years at the community college, she'd gone out some. After that, her mother had been so sick Caitlin hadn't been interested in a social life. Then her mother had died, and Caitlin hadn't cared about dating.

But the thought of dating again suddenly appealed to her. Oh, not with anyone like Brent who was looking to settle down. But maybe with someone who wanted to go to dinner, go dancing, go to plays. Assuming Mason really was a nice guy, he might be a good choice.

''They have a few national papers,'' she said, nodding toward the shelf where the newspapers were located. ''And of course, the daily papers from Dallas, Fort Worth, and Shreveport. Will any of those do?''

Mason leaned forward until his mouth was dangerously close to her ear. ''You've saved my life, Caitlin Rogers. The least I can do is take you to dinner tomorrow night.''

Caitlin studied him. ''Dinner?''

Mason smiled. ''Yeah. If there isn't a decent place around here, we can drive to Tyler. I know a couple of good restaurants there.''

She'd just been thinking about going out with Mason, but now that he'd asked, she hesitated. She didn't know this man.

"I'd like to know you a little longer than five minutes before I agree to a date," she admitted.

Rather than looking offended, Mason said, "But you already know I'm related to Vanda. Doesn't that help?"

Caitlin would certainly ask Vanda about Mason. But the recommendation of a loving relative didn't mean anything.

"It helps some." An idea occurred to her, and she smiled. "Of course, we could meet for dinner at the café two doors down. Then I'd have a chance to get to know you—"

"While staying on home turf," he finished. "You are a very cautious woman. But I guess I either do it your way or no way, so dinner at the café sounds fine. Just to show you how harmless I am, I'll bring Vanda with me so she can tell you I'm safe. Then, if you're not nervous, maybe we can drop Vanda at home and go out for a drink after dinner. Does that work?"

Caitlin couldn't see how he could be more reasonable. And it did mean a lot to her that he was willing to adjust. So why was she hesitating? Why didn't she just say yes? Even if she went to dinner with Mason, and even if she went with him for a drink later, that didn't mean she had to do anything else. Plus, she really did need a little fun and excitement in her life, and she had to start somewhere.

He was still looking at her, so Caitlin said, "Okay. Sure. I guess you can't be any fairer than that, right?"

"Fair? I've never had a woman call a date with me

fair, but I'll take what I can get. So how about we meet for dinner tomorrow at the café at nine?"

He sure didn't know much about a small town. "Nine is kind of late for dinner in Desmond. In fact, I'm pretty sure that's when the café closes. How about six instead?"

Mason made a face. "Six? You're kidding, right? I've barely had lunch by six."

Caitlin couldn't help smiling at his pained expression. Mason Gibbs had big city written all over him, and although she didn't consider herself a hick, the two of them obviously didn't have much in common. Still, differences could be overcome. "How about seven?"

Leaning toward her, he gave her what she had to guess was his lady-killer grin. Even objectively, it was a good one. Just enough of a touch of the devil to catch her attention. "Sure. Seven sounds fine."

His penetrating look made her feel self-conscious, so Caitlin decided now would be a really good time to go back to her table. "See you then."

Still smiling at Mason, she backed up a couple of steps, then spun around. And found herself face-to-face with Brent.

Brent had known deep in his bones Mason Gibbs would run into Caitlin. Hell, he'd practically sent the creep right to her. Although he'd bet a guy like Gibbs probably found the prettiest woman in every town he visited. When Brent had seen the red Corvette still parked in front of the library when he'd pulled in, he'd known instinctively that he'd find Gibbs hitting on Caitlin.

He just hadn't expected to walk in and find her so receptive to the guy's advances.

"Hello, Caitlin." Brent nodded at Mason Gibbs. "See you found the library." It took all of his self-control not to pull Caitlin away from the man.

When Caitlin looked at him, a faint blush covered her cheeks. He'd loved to know if it was because she was upset he'd caught her flirting with Gibbs, or whether the other man was the cause of the faint pink tint on her cheeks.

"You two know each other?" she asked, her gaze meeting Brent's briefly and then skirting away.

"Oh, yes. This nice officer gave me a ticket on my way into town. Sorta his way of saying welcome." Mason had a smug smile on his pretty boy face.

Brent would give anything to wipe that smile off. As soon as the thought went through his mind, he pulled himself up short. What was wrong with him? He didn't have a claim on Caitlin. Still, that didn't mean he wanted to see her take up with this jackass.

"Mason, my father is the chief of police here in Desmond. Brent was just doing his job," Caitlin said.

Foolishly, perhaps even childishly, Brent was thrilled to hear Caitlin take his side. And a little part of him wondered if Mason might change his mind about her now that he knew who her father was.

Sure enough, the smile on the other man's face faded slightly. "Let me get this straight—your old man is the head of the local police department?"

Brent leaned against one of the tables, enjoying this more than he should. Crossing his arms, he studied Mason Gibbs. Expensive clothes. Expensive haircut. Expensive watch. If Caitlin seriously didn't want a relationship, she'd picked the right guy. Mason Gibbs looked like the king of the one-night stands.

And it made Brent's blood run cold. Especially

since Gibbs was looking at Caitlin as if she were a cut of prime rib and he hadn't eaten in a month.

"Yes." Caitlin glanced at him and then back to Mason. "My father is the chief."

There was a resigned note in her voice, and Brent realized she expected Mason to take off at a run. To give the guy credit, he didn't. He simply shrugged. "Okay with me unless he's got a nasty temper."

Caitlin smiled, and Brent felt his gut clench when she directed her smile to the other man. "Great. So we're still on for tomorrow?"

"You bet." Mason shot a cautious glance at Brent, then said, "I think I'll go bother Aunt Vanda for a while."

Moving forward, Mason put his hand on Caitlin's arm and leaned toward her. With a start, Brent realized the man meant to kiss her.

"Caitlin." Unconsciously, Brent moved forward to stop him. He was almost at Caitlin's side when he stopped, surprised by his own action. He'd surprised Caitlin and Mason, too. They both turned to look at him. And something in his expression must have finally convinced Mason Gibbs to back off. He dropped his hand, muttered a quick good-bye to Caitlin, and then took off.

Caitlin turned and watched him disappear. Once he was gone, Brent waited for her to shift her attention back to him. He knew she was mad. He'd known her long enough to recognize the stubborn set to her shoulders. And maybe he deserved her anger. Hell, he didn't know up from down anymore. Certainly not around Caitlin. All he knew was he wanted the best for her, and as far as he could tell, the best wasn't Mason Gibbs.

Caitlin turned and faced him. After a quick look around the library, she walked toward him, her balled fists planted on her hips.

"What was with the bodyguard routine, Brent?"

"I don't know what you're talking about."

With a sigh, she said, "You were standing there looking like my own personal protector. You may want to settle down in Desmond and raise a family, but I don't. Mason Gibbs is exactly the type of man I should be dating. Someone who isn't interested in forever."

"Caitlin, that man isn't interested in tomorrow morning."

The annoyance in her eyes was unnerving. "How do you know? And even if that's true, what business is it of yours? Everyone in this town is always so certain they know what's best for me, but they don't. Butt out, Brent. I'm not telling you how to live your life."

She was right. He knew she was right. "I'm not trying to push you around."

Tipping her head, she met his gaze, the shine in her pretty eyes making him wonder if she was fighting back tears. He felt lower than a gopher's belly.

"Yes, you are." She said each word slowly, distinctly.

He emphatically shook his head. "No. I'm worried about you. That's different."

"Well, don't worry about me. I can handle myself."

He wanted to believe that. He really did. Caitlin was the most independent woman he'd ever known. She was resourceful. Decisive. Intuitive.

But he couldn't help feeling she was a babe in the woods when it came to men. He drew nearer, the enticing scent of her perfume filling his senses, and he wondered about the wisdom of his actions. But he had to do this. He had to make certain she was safe.

"Caitlin, I—"

"Stop." She moved, just a tiny bit, but it was enough to place her directly in front of him. Close enough to touch. And he realized if he bent his head, she was also close enough to kiss. And he wanted to. Very much.

"We have to ignore this thing happening between us, Brent. It can't go anywhere. It's just chemistry and"—she waved one hand in the air—"illusion. I'm wrong for you. You're wrong for me. That's that."

Her voice was a mere whisper, and Brent leaned toward her to catch her words. He lowered his own voice. "Okay, but I don't think going out with someone like Mason Gibbs is right for you either." He brushed a strand of hair away from her cheek, his fingers lingering against the softness of her skin. "You deserve so much better."

Her gaze moved across his face, finally landing on his lips. Need overwhelmed him. Without thinking, he did what he'd wanted to do ever since he'd given her the brief kiss at her party. He dipped his head and found her lips with his.

Wrapping his arms around her, passion rushed through his veins like a wildfire. Rational thought flew out the window, and he backed her against the shelves, his tongue slipping inside her mouth, his hands molding her against him.

Lust ran through his blood like an elixir as his tongue met hers. She murmured something against his mouth, but he couldn't understand her. He started to pull away, but she moaned and pressed closer to him, kissing him with equal hunger.

Damn. . . .

Laughter from some other part of the library finally pulled him back to reality. He broke the kiss, lifting his head away from her, dropping his arms from around her tempting body. As he struggled to catch his breath, he looked at her. He saw confusion in her eyes, and knew he'd put it there.

"I shouldn't have done that," he admitted, knowing he'd only made things worse.

"Of course you shouldn't have. I shouldn't have either." Her breathless voice was almost his undoing. "We have to stop kissing, touching. I'm not going to change my mind, Brent. I'm leaving at the end of the month."

"I know that."

She studied him closely before saying, "Then I think we should stop kissing. Now let's go. Mabel's probably wondering why we're late."

With care, she straightened her dress and walked away, leaving him standing there. She was right. He shouldn't have kissed her, but the temptation had been too strong.

Brent rubbed a tired hand across his face. He'd come back to Desmond looking for a simpler life. One thing he knew for certain—kissing Caitlin wasn't going to make his life any simpler. Not by a long shot.

Chapter Four

Mabel Dawson flipped through the pages of the books Caitlin had brought and smiled her gratitude. "These books should be a big help in my search. Thank you, dear."

The annoying gene for truthfulness in Caitlin's DNA forced her to say, "You know, Mrs. Dawson, there's a chance you may not be related to European royalty, but if Desmond, Texas, had royalty, you'd certainly be a duchess or baroness."

"Or a princess?" The older woman smiled brightly. "I think I'd rather like being a princess."

Caitlin returned her smile. Mabel Dawson had lived in Desmond her entire life. If anyone deserved to be a princess, this lady did.

"I see no reason why you couldn't be a princess. You taught fifth grade for most of the town's population. That deserves princess status at the very least."

Glancing at Brent, she caught him grinning. "Don't you agree, Brent?"

"Absolutely."

Mabel laughed. "You two are full of hooey. But I appreciate the thought anyway. Still, I think I'll do a little more research on European royalty first."

While Mabel began to read one of the books, Caitlin and Brent headed to the kitchen to put away the food they'd brought. When they both reached for the handle of the refrigerator at the same time, Caitlin jumped as Brent accidentally brushed against her. Talk about skittish. She'd always been relaxed and comfortable around Brent. One little bone-melting, toe-curling, life-shaking kiss, and she was a bundle of nerves. She needed to put what had happened in perspective.

"Sorry," she muttered, not really certain what she was apologizing for but knowing she felt pretty darn sorry anyway.

Brent set the last of the food on the narrow shelf in the old refrigerator, shut the door, then turned to face her.

"You don't have to say you're sorry, but I'd appreciate if you wouldn't act like I'm going to attack you. I know I shouldn't have kissed you at the library, but it . . . happened. I can't let it ruin our friendship."

He was right. She knew he was right, so to prove a point more to herself than to him, Caitlin took the two necessary steps to stand directly in front of him. She ignored her own excitement at his nearness and focused instead on the importance of the job at hand.

She kept her voice low but firm as she said, "I don't want it to ruin our friendship either. I promise, I'll stop being so jumpy. But I meant what I said at the library. No more kissing. It confuses everything."

"I couldn't agree more." Brent moved around her. "Why don't we put it behind us, and go visit with Mabel?"

Caitlin studied his face. He looked as determined as she felt, which was a good thing. They truly needed to put that kiss behind them. They had a lot of important things to do before she left town. So it was terrific that Brent wanted to forget the kiss. Really terrific.

Absolutely terrific.

Arrgh. Why in the world did she feel so disappointed that he'd agreed so quickly?

She knew the answer to that one—because she was a lunatic in search of an asylum, that's why. She had to force herself to think clearly on this subject. Okay, so being around Brent blasted her hormones into the stratosphere, but she had to ignore those feelings. That was lust. Simple animal attraction. Nothing more. And as soon as she moved to Dallas, all of those feelings would disappear like raindrops on a summer sidewalk.

Brent was still waiting by the doorway to the kitchen, looking at her expectantly. Caitlin smiled at him, and was relieved when he smiled back. If she tried really, really hard, maybe she could get their friendship back on track.

Walking past him, she inwardly congratulated herself when she didn't jump when he patted her shoulder. She could do this. She was a smart, strong woman. All she needed to do was focus. She glanced back at him, and he flashed her a crooked grin, his brown eyes filled with humor.

She tried to focus—unsuccessfully—and it occurred to her that a football stadium full of self-control wouldn't hurt, either.

Brent looked down from the roof of the McKinleys' house and grinned. Only Caitlin Rogers could have talked him back up on a roof. When he'd been in high school and college, he'd worked on construction crews to pay the bills. But the day he'd graduated from college, he'd vowed never to climb up on a roof again. He'd baked in the hot sun for the very last time. At least he thought he had.

Just went to show you what a pretty smile from an even prettier woman could make a guy do.

"How's it coming?" Caitlin hollered up from the ground.

Brent glanced behind him at the two other people on the roof with him. Now these guys knew what they were doing. The Patterson brothers, Phil and Bill, ran a roofing company. A busy roofing company. But somehow, Caitlin had convinced them to donate an entire afternoon of their time and fix this roof for free.

"Tell her we're doing great," Bill yelled over to Brent. "If those thunderstorms hold off for another couple of hours, we should make it."

Brent relayed the message down to Caitlin, who he could tell was still annoyed they hadn't let her join them on the roof. Bill and Phil had insisted, though, that no one could come up on the roof who didn't have experience walking one. Their rule had turned out to be non-negotiable.

Just his luck he'd spent enough time on roofs to

know how to keep from falling on his butt. That had garnered him the privilege of frying once again in the relentless Texas sun. At this particular moment, he felt like a marshmallow at a cookout.

"I'm not sure you guys are going to make it. The storms are coming fast," Caitlin said. "I think I should come up to help. I'll be very careful."

Before she took two steps toward the ladder, Bill and Phil both yelled, "No!"

Then Bill added, "We're not having you run around up here and getting hurt, Caitlin, and that's final."

To soften the verdict, Brent added, "They won't even let me do much because it's been a while since I was up this high. Don't worry. They're making good progress, Caitlin. We should beat the rainstorm."

Caitlin stood on the ground, her hands on her hips, staring up at him. He knew this was killing her. Caitlin was a hands-on kind of person, and standing by and watching was driving her nuts. She was always right in the middle of all the activity. Frustration practically emanated from her, yet she didn't complain. Not Caitlin. She was way too nice to voice her frustration.

Which was another thing he liked about her. In fact, when it came right down to it, he couldn't remember ever meeting anyone he respected more than Caitlin Rogers.

He ought to wrap the lady in bright yellow danger tape, because that's what she was to him—dangerous. Good old-fashioned lust he could handle. He could at least try to turn it off. But how did you stop admiring someone? Talk about something that was damn near impossible.

Turning his attention back to the work at hand,

Brent had to admit, Caitlin managed to work miracles around town. Since their initial visit to Mabel Dawson yesterday, they'd also delivered meals to a shut-in, helped a homeless family find a place to stay, and now they were fixing the roof on an elderly couple's house before a bad rainstorm set in.

As far as he could tell, Caitlin could do anything. Everyone in town loved her, and he understood why. She had a heart of gold. Caring for others, giving to others seemed to come naturally to her, so people loved her. He just had to make certain he didn't fall *in* love with her. That would be a lot more deadly than hanging up here on this broken roof.

When Caitlin asked again if she could come up and help, Phil looked at Brent and said with a laugh, "Tell her we'll send you down to tie her up if she tries coming up here. I'm not going to let the police chief's daughter run around on a roof. If she fell, everyone in Desmond would ride me and Bill out of town on a rail."

Bill stopped hammering at the sound of his name and grinned at his brother and Brent. "You have to love Caitlin, though. There's nothing I wouldn't do for her." The older man's face reflected his determination. "Wish she weren't moving away to Dallas."

Phil grunted his agreement, then gave Brent a pointed look. "Can't you think of a way to change her mind? Seems to me if he wanted to, a young guy like you could come up with a thing or two."

Hey. What was going on here? Phil and Bill were both confirmed bachelors. They ought to be the last guys to try and sell him on romance.

"Caitlin really wants to move to Dallas," Brent said. "She has a great job lined up there. I think everyone who cares about her should be happy she has this opportunity."

Bill snorted. "We're happy for her. We just don't want her to go."

Phil lowered his voice and added, "Brent, why don't you woo her?"

Okay, this had gone far enough. Moving away from the edge of the roof so he was certain Caitlin wouldn't hear him, he turned and faced the brothers. "I appreciate that the town is going to miss her, but I'm not going to try to change her mind. She deserves this chance, and we should be supportive."

That got them. The brothers nodded sadly. "Yeah, you're right," Bill said with a heavy sigh. "We should. But it's kinda hard since we're going to miss her so damn much."

Brent had meant what he'd said. He could tell how much Caitlin meant to everyone lucky enough to know her. But she still deserved the chance to have her dreams come true. She'd done so much to make everyone around her happy. Now it was her turn.

"To tell you the truth, I'm hoping that something happens to make Caitlin change her mind." Phil looked at his brother. "Come on, let's get this roof done before that rain comes or she'll climb up here and try to finish the job herself."

Brent knew the brothers really hadn't dropped the subject, but he let it go. Poor Caitlin. She ran into this everywhere she went. No one wanted her to leave Desmond for the bright lights of Dallas.

And as much as he hated to admit it, he was every bit as bad as everyone else. He didn't want her to go, either. She drew him to her, so much so that when he climbed down the ladder an hour later to gather some more materials, he made a point of seeking her out.

"How's it going?" Caitlin asked him as she helped him collect supplies.

"Okay. Bill and Phil have kicked into overdrive, so I think we're going to make it with time to spare."

"Great." The radiant smile she gave him made his heart beat faster. She was a beautiful woman, both inside and out. Like everyone else in town, he was going to miss her. Maybe even more after that killer kiss. They might have agreed to forget about it, but passion like that tended to linger in your mind.

"It will be another Good Neighbors success story," he said. "You do good things with this organization."

"It's nothing special," she said.

But it was. And Good Neighbors only succeeded because Caitlin was a special woman. Sweet. Caring. And way too sexy for his peace of mind. If only she could find her dreams in Desmond, things would be different.

But she didn't want what he wanted, so he took a step back from her. Of course, that didn't mean he was happy she was going out with Mason Gibbs tonight. Caitlin might not be the right woman for him, but she deserved a lot better than that jerk.

"The people of this town do all the work for Good Neighbors," she said, refilling his water bottle and handing it back to him. "I like helping folks, and I don't do that much. Today, I'm not doing anything, just standing here fretting. You and the Pattersons are doing all the work."

Brent chuckled. "Don't count me in on that. I'm only allowed to fetch things for Bill and Phil. They won't let me do anything. I'm more like a trained dog than an assistant."

"Still, you're up there. And the McKinleys really appreciate the help." She glanced at the roof and then back at him. Her blue eyes met his. "Thank you, Brent."

"For what?"

"Taking over Good Neighbors."

"You've thanked me already." As he stood looking at her, Brent felt a crazy sensation of rightness fill him. At that moment, he was like everyone else in Desmond—there wasn't anything he wouldn't do for Caitlin. "I don't think I'll do half the job you've done. You have a real flair for this."

She smiled at him again. "Of course you will. You'll be great. And Good Neighbors pretty much runs itself. You'll have no trouble keeping it going."

"Aren't you going to miss it?"

The smile on her face dimmed. "Sure. A little." At his dubious look, she added, "Okay, a lot. But since I'll know you're taking care of everything, it won't be so bad. Besides, I'll be doing lots of good things at the Henderson Charity. I'm so lucky they gave me the job."

He didn't believe her for a second. Her wistful expression gave her away, but he didn't challenge her. Instead, he simply said, "They aren't giving you a thing. You've more than earned that job. And if you ask me, the Henderson Charity has no idea how lucky they are to get you."

With that, Brent turned and headed back to the ladder. He had to get back up on the roof to finish the job before the rain came. Sure, he knew the Mc-

Kinleys appreciated his help. But that's not why he climbed the ladder.

He did it for Caitlin.

"Come on, admit it," Mason prompted, leaning across the table. "You're having fun."

How could one man be so dumb? "You've got to be kidding. I'm not having fun." Caitlin glanced around the small nightclub. She shouldn't have come here with Mason. She should have called it a night after dinner. Jeez. She must be as dumb as her date, because she'd thought a night out would help erase the memory of that amazing kiss Brent had given her in the library yesterday. At least she'd hoped it would.

All day long, she'd been thinking about that blasted, glorious, terrible, wonderful kiss. The man could kiss, no two ways around it. Brent's kiss had more than rocked her world. That kiss had shaken, rattled, and rolled her equilibrium. For her own peace of mind, she needed to forget all about it. Wipe it from her mind. Stop thinking about it, stop reliving the sensations it had evoked.

Unfortunately, Mason Gibbs wasn't the man to make her forget. Heck, he wasn't much of anything, based on her time spent with him so far. The bottom line was, the man had turned into a jerk the second they'd dropped his aunt off at her house. All through dinner, Vanda had made it clear she thought the world of her nephew. Caitlin wasn't really surprised, because as dinner progressed she came to realize that Mason Gibbs could be very charming.

Charming enough to get her to agree to go to a club in Tyler after dinner. Charming enough to convince her that, rather than take two cars, she should leave her car at home. Mason had dropped Vanda off at her house and then picked Caitlin up in her driveway. While she'd waited for him to show up, she kept glancing at Brent's house. It had been dark. Maybe he was out on a date, too.

That thought had troubled her as Mason had driven to Tyler, the closest big city. He'd picked a small club he claimed to know well, and then—drink after drink—had transformed into a major bozo.

So now here she was, over an hour away from home with no car, with a date who was becoming increasingly drunk.

Great. Just great.

When Mason muttered something about getting another drink, Caitlin decided to take things into her own hands. "We're leaving now."

Without waiting for his response, she stood and picked up her purse. Giving Mason a direct look, she hoped he had enough good sense left to know she wasn't kidding. But good sense seemed to be something foreign to this man. He reached over and patted her hip in a too-familiar gesture. Caitlin swatted his hand away.

"Sure, babe. I get it. You want to be alone with me." He winked.

Caitlin groaned. She'd rather be tossed naked into a rattlesnake pit. "Oh, no. I want to go home now, and I'm going to drive because you're too drunk."

How could she have been stupid enough to come here with Mason? She should have known he was all wrong for her. The only excuse she could come up with was that she hadn't been thinking clearly. She'd been feeling discombobulated by Brent's kiss, and she'd made a stupid mistake. But that mistake was about to be corrected—quickly.

Mason hollered for the bill, then argued that he was sober enough to drive. Caitlin refused to give in. The amount of alcohol he'd consumed was well over the legal limit. No way was she letting him drive. After Mason finished paying, she stuck out her hand, waiting for his keys. He treated her to a few choice curses, but in the end, he didn't put up much of a fight. He dug the car keys out of the pocket of his jeans and tossed them on the table.

Gritting her teeth, Caitlin picked them up. She led the way out of the club, not really caring if Mason followed her or not. But he did. She could hear him mumbling behind her and she was thankful he didn't give her any problems. He just slid into the passenger's seat.

"You sure you can handle all the power of this car?" Mason asked. "This 'vette really hauls." Then he added in a mocking tone, "I wouldn't want you to get scared."

"I can drive it," Caitlin said dryly as she climbed into the driver's seat, moved it forward, then adjusted the mirrors. When she was certain she felt familiar with the car, she fastened her seat belt. "Buckle up."

Mason leaned over, placing one hand on her upper thigh. "Why don't you buckle it for me, babe?"

That was it. Caitlin shoved on Mason's chest, pushing him back into his own seat.

"Listen to me, Mason. I'm the police chief's daughter. Don't think for a second that I don't know how to handle myself. If you touch me again, I'll break your hand." She waited a couple of seconds for her words to seep into his liquor-fogged brain. "Now do you get me?"

Mason paled a little and satisfaction filled Caitlin. Totally subdued now, he silently buckled his seat belt, then leaned his head on the headrest. Before Caitlin even reached Interstate 20 to head back to Desmond, Mason was sound asleep.

As she drove, she fought back her anger. How in the world was she going to get home after she dropped off this bozo? Vanda didn't drive, and Caitlin wouldn't drive herself home in Mason's car. Moreover, she couldn't—no, she wouldn't—call her father or one of her brothers. They would go bananas if they found out about this.

And her girlfriends were all married. Most of them had children. She could hardly disturb their families at one o'clock in the morning.

Caitlin knew the answer to her problem but hated to face it. The only choice was Brent, but jeez, how could she call him? He'd already made it clear what he thought of Mason Gibbs. Calling him would only prove him right. But she didn't have any options unless she wanted to camp out on Vanda's front lawn or take her chances walking home this late at night. Talk about being stuck between the devil and the deep blue sea.

She chose the devil. After she pulled the Corvette into Vanda's driveway, she dug her cell phone out of her purse and dialed. Brent answered on the first ring, almost as if he'd been sitting at home, waiting to hear from her.

"Hello." Brent's voice was clear, wide-awake. Considering how hard he'd worked up on that roof today, she was surprised he hadn't been asleep. Again, she wondered if he'd waited up for her, but she quickly dismissed the thought. Surely Brent had better things to do than worry about her.

Still, it was an intriguing thought, but it didn't make what she had to ask any easier. "Brent, I hate to bother—"

"What happened? Are you all right?"

"I'm fine." Caitlin stared into the dark night. She hated this, truly hated it. But none of her other options appealed to her, either. Might as well get it over with. Sucking in a deep breath, she hurriedly said, "Could you possibly come pick me up?"

"Of course. Where?"

His calm voice helped restore her dignity a little. There was no censure in it, just worry. "Vanda's house."

"I'll be there in ten minutes."

He was there in seven. When she saw his headlights, Caitlin climbed out of the Corvette. He stopped his Suburban in front of Vanda's house and shut off the engine.

Caitlin walked over to meet him, figuring the sooner she got this over with, the sooner she could forget about tonight. "I'm really sorry about this," she said quietly when he got out of his car. "Mason had too much to drink, and I had to drive us back from Tyler. My car is at my apartment, so I have no way to get home."

For several tense moments, Brent stood next to his Suburban, simply looking at her. She wished she could see his face better, but clouds obscured the moon, and the light from the lone street lamp was too faint to make out much other than the fact that he was frowning. Finally he said, "Are you sure you're all right?"

Caitlin could practically feel tension emanating from him. She'd rarely seen this side of Brent, but it was obvious he was very upset. Lightly touching his arm, she said, "I'm fine. Really. But I can't get Mason inside the house. He weighs too much, and I don't think it's safe to let him sleep out here in the car."

Brent walked past her to Mason's Corvette. With one swift yank, he opened the passenger's door and pulled Mason to his feet. "Go inside," he ordered in a no-nonsense voice.

Caitlin really didn't expect Brent's command to have an effect, but it did. Mason gave her a lopsided grin, then stumbled more than once as he made his way across the yard and up the steps to the front door. When it became obvious he was too drunk to fit his key into the lock, Brent muttered a colorful curse and sprinted up the steps. He grabbed the key from Mason and unlocked the door.

"Relock this once you're inside. I don't want Vanda having any trouble because you left her front door unlocked," he said to Mason, who did as he was told. A couple of seconds after the front door shut, Brent came down the steps and over to Caitlin.

Wordlessly, he walked with her to his Suburban, opening the passenger door. Caitlin moved past him and climbed inside his car. After he shut her door, she watched him walk around the front of the car to the driver's side. For the first time, she noticed how nicely he was dressed. A nice shirt. Nice pants. These weren't clothes he'd thrown on in the middle of the night when he'd gotten her phone call. So had he been waiting up to make sure she got home okay? Or had he just gotten home from his own date?

When he started the car, the light from the dash illuminated his handsome features a little. He didn't look as upset as he'd been earlier. Still, she felt compelled to apologize.

"I feel like an idiot, so go ahead and call me one if you'd like," she admitted, wanting to break the silence between them. "I know you said that Mason wasn't a good guy. I should have listened."

"None of this is your fault. It's his. Don't take his blame."

Leave it to Brent to try to make her feel better. But she didn't. "Still, I dragged you out in the middle of the night—"

"I didn't mind."

Caitlin turned slightly in her seat so she could look at him. "Go on. Say it. Get it over with. The suspense is killing me."

He glanced at her briefly, then returned his gaze to the road. "Say what?"

"Whatever it is you want to say, and don't try to convince me you're not dying to say something. I know you're angry with Mason, and rightfully so. I'm really mad, too."

"The guy's an ass." Brent turned the Suburban into his driveway, circling around to the rear of the house and parked inside his garage. The overhead light was on, and for the first time tonight, she could see him clearly. He looked upset, and she felt badly about that.

He shoved open his door and then glanced at her. "Come on, I'll walk you home."

The hollow tone in his voice got to her, and she

put her hand on his arm, stopping him from climbing out. "Brent, I really am sorry. I guess I should have known he was a jerk, but he seemed so . . ." She shrugged. "He seemed nice enough at dinner. And Vanda had nothing but wonderful things to say about him. Plus, when things turned bad, I handled the situation. I drove us home."

Brent looked away from her. "Yeah. That was smart. But I can't help wondering what will happen when you live in Dallas. Who will you call if you need help?"

His comment irritated her. "Okay, I'll admit that Mason isn't exactly the poster boy for nice like I'd expected, but I deserve more credit than you're giving me. I'm not a child, Brent. I can take care of myself."

"I know you're not a child. I'm worried about you, that's all. That guy could have . . ." He met and held her gaze. "He could have hurt you."

The sincerity and concern in his voice made her anger fade. Brent wasn't trying to be her big brother. He was just a good guy who didn't want to see something bad happen to her. And, if she didn't know better, there also seemed to be more than a trace of jealousy in his voice.

"Mason didn't do anything to me other than really annoy me," she reassured him. "I was fine. And I'll be fine in Dallas, too." She tipped her head, studying him. He was obviously still upset. Hoping to tease him into a good mood, she nudged him with her elbow and said, "Guess I'm going to have to pay you off so you won't tell Dad or the boys about tonight."

An odd light flashed in his dark eyes. "Now you know I'd never tell. I never told on you when we were growing up, and back then, I had a lot more I could tell about."

She laughed. "Yeah, come to think of it, you do have a lot of blackmail material on me. Thank goodness you're so honorable, or Dad would have grounded me for life a long time ago."

Brent smiled that sexy half smile of his, and Caitlin drew in a deep breath. The man was so handsome, and genuinely nice, and seriously tempting that she completely lost her ability to make small talk. And as he continued to look at her, it only got worse. Oh, boy. Desire was getting the better of her, and she knew her ability to handle this situation logically was fading faster than a vacation tan.

Brent's gaze was intent. What was he thinking? Did he feel the same need she did? The same heat that was coursing through her veins? Brent was the wrong man at the wrong time, but that message didn't seem to be reaching her body. Right. Wrong. It didn't seem to matter once her hormones kicked in.

"So you think I'm honorable?" he asked.

His husky voice only made her heart beat faster. The chemistry was bubbling between them again. Strong. Urgent. She knew he felt it, too. It was in his gaze, his darkened eyes that watched her closely. But she could escape if she wanted to. Brent wouldn't stop her.

She stayed where she was.

"Yes. I think you're honorable." The words came out as a mere whisper in the silence of the car. Clearing her throat, she added, "That's why you came for me tonight. That's why you won't tell my father and brothers. I want you to know how much I appreciate your friendship. I've always appreciated it."

Without considering the wisdom of her actions, or perhaps because she wanted to tempt fate, Caitlin leaned across and dropped a kiss on his cheek. "You're sweet and a terrific buddy."

When she moved away from him, he said softly, "I'm not feeling like your buddy right now, Caitlin."

Her heart skipped a few beats. With effort, she tried to keep her voice steady as she asked, "You're not?"

"No." Reaching out, he ran the back of his hand down the side of her face, his gaze still holding her own. "Tell me again why being close is a bad idea. Why we shouldn't kiss each other until we both forget our own names."

Truthfully, she was having a hard time remembering the reasons herself at this moment. Right now, she could almost taste his lips on hers, almost feel his arms holding her close. Her gaze dropped to his firm lips. She wanted his kiss, desperately, and when he leaned toward her, she eagerly met him halfway.

Oh, yeah. This was what she'd wanted all day.

Chapter Five

Kissing Caitlin was a really bad idea, but Brent couldn't help himself. He'd longed to hold her all day, and he wasn't about to pass up this chance now.

As much as he could within the close confines of his car, he shifted nearer to her, his hands skimming her sweet body. His lips grazed hers once, twice, tasting her passion, mixing it with his own. Apparently, his slow pace frustrated her, because she murmured something he didn't catch, then parted her lips and wrapped her arms around his neck.

For a heartbeat, he hesitated. He still had enough common sense to know this was theoretically wrong. But it *felt* so very right that soon desire fogged his brain until he no longer cared if he damned his own soul. By degrees, reason slipped away and he deepened the kiss.

Caitlin tasted like pure heaven. When his tongue

touched hers, she moaned slightly and pressed against him harder. Desire pounded through his veins. He wanted her. Here. Now. He cupped her upturned face in his hands.

Their need for each other intensified. Soul-stirring kisses blended one into the next. Unable to restrain himself, Brent slid one hand off her shoulder and took the luscious weight of a tender breast in his palm. At the contact, Caitlin sighed into his mouth. Through the thin cotton of her T-shirt, he felt her nipple harden.

"I want you," he muttered as he dropped kisses down the side of her neck, then felt like kicking himself. Talk about finesse. He'd handled that with all the aplomb of a seventeen-year-old.

"I want you, too." Her voice, although sultry with need, was tinged with sadness.

Reluctantly, Brent lifted his head and looked at her. Desire and remorse warred within him. "I'm sorry," he said, then added, "It seems like I spend most of my time telling you I'm sorry for kissing you. But you know, I'm not really sorry at all."

As he waited for her reaction, anxiety coiled through him like a snake. Finally, Caitlin broke the tension by laughing softly.

"You're right. I'm not sorry, either. What a kiss. Wow!" She moved away from him, returning to her side of the car. Her voice was light as she said, "But we've got to figure out a way to deal with this, um, attraction. I mean, some other way rather than simply giving into it. As far as I can tell, that's all we've tried up to this point."

Only Caitlin could make him see the humor in this situation. He ran one hand around the back of his neck, kneading the tight muscles. Then he grinned at her. "Yeah. I know. We're failing miserably. Any ideas?"

Caitlin looked away from him, glancing instead through the windshield of the car. "I'm fresh out. My plan of dating someone else to get my mind off you didn't work."

Her comment confused him. "You went out with Mason just to short-circuit this attraction between us?" Although he knew he shouldn't, he liked that idea.

"Yes. No." She waved one hand. "Maybe. But since he turned out to be a jerk, it didn't work." With a dramatic sigh, she finally looked at him and rolled her eyes. "Brent, this is all your fault. You make it difficult for me to concentrate on Good Neighbors. Or anything else, for that matter. When you keep kissing me, it only confuses me."

"I don't mean to confuse you," was all he could think to say. Then, unable to stop himself, he pointed out, "And for the record, you kissed me first this time."

She tipped up her chin just a fraction, and Brent almost smiled. This was the Caitlin he recognized. The sassy Caitlin who he'd grown up with.

"I gave you a friendly little peck on the cheek. You gave me a bone-melting kiss in return," she said, shoving open the car door. "I was being friendly. You were being . . . horny."

Brent chuckled, glad they'd cooled things down between them. When she got out of the car, he did, too. He had to admit, her comment intrigued him. Needing to satisfy his curiosity, he asked, "You thought it was bone-melting, huh?"

Caitlin frowned at him. "You're missing the point."

"Which is?"

"We can't get involved. We're all wrong for each other, and kissing each other doesn't help."

Brent knew she was right, so he gave her the only answer he had. "I can't seem to help myself."

She slowly shook her head, then gave him a small smile. There was nothing even remotely seductive about her smile, yet it still made his hormones take off. "Brent, we both need to try harder, that's all. Sure, I understand tonight's kiss. We were both upset. That's why we gave into temptation."

He groaned. "You don't really believe that, do you?"

She looked genuinely perplexed. "Sure. It's been a long night."

His laugh contained no humor. "That's not why I kissed you. I kissed you because you're a beautiful woman, Caitlin, and I find you sexy as hell."

"Well, don't."

"Don't what?"

"Find me sexy as hell. Snap out of it."

Oh, now that was funny. And also easier said than done. Whether she meant it or not, Caitlin was driving him crazy. He rubbed his face with his hands and took a couple of steps toward the open garage door. "Why don't I walk you home then?"

"That's probably the best idea," she said. Silently, they walked out of the garage, down his driveway, and across to her house. When they reached the steps leading to the apartment over her father's garage, Brent stopped.

Caitlin glanced at him over her shoulder.

"I'll stand here until you go inside," he said.

"Fine." Caitlin climbed the first step, then stopped.

She turned to face him. With the added benefit of the step, she was closer to eye level with him. "Thank you."

At first he thought she was thanking him for the kiss, but then he realized what an idiot he was. She was thanking him for the ride tonight. "No problem."

She continued to look at him, the dim outdoor lighting making it difficult for him to make out what she was thinking. Tension arced between them, so strong it practically crackled. But underneath that was the feeling of friendship they'd always had. Whatever ended up happening between them, he would always like and care about Caitlin.

Brent cleared his throat, willing his heart to stop slamming against his ribs. "Have a good night, Caitlin."

She gave him the tiniest of smiles. "You, too."

After she'd walked inside her apartment and locked the door behind her, Brent headed home. Tonight hadn't helped anything. . . . In fact, things were more confused than ever. Nonetheless, only one thought kept circling through his mind.

Caitlin had called their kiss bone-melting. That interesting comment would probably keep him awake half the night.

She and Brent were playing with fire, Caitlin decided the next day as she left the small grocery store in the center of town. Yep. No doubt about it. If they weren't careful, they'd both get burned. Badly.

The problem was, she didn't know what to do about the situation. She couldn't simply avoid Brent until she moved, because he worked with her almost every day on Good Neighbors. And when she was around him, she had no luck turning off the red-hot attraction between them. They needed a plan. A good, solid, foolproof plan.

Unfortunately, she couldn't think of one. As she walked to her car in the hot summer sun, she yawned. Maybe a nap would help her put this all in perspective. Since she and Brent had given in to this craziness, she hadn't been sleeping well. Maybe that's why she couldn't come up with a plan—her brain was simply too tired. A little sleep and she'd probably be dazzled by her own brilliance.

But before she could take a nap, she needed to head back over to the small office Good Neighbors occupied in the city hall. There was paperwork to be done, and a few details to tie up.

Darn that Brent Stewart. Her sleeplessness was all his fault. Well, sort of. Every time Brent kissed her, he got her too riled up to sleep well. He needed to—

"Caitlin. Hi, Caitlin."

Caitlin shifted the bag of groceries she carried and looked around. From across the street, she could see Mary Beth Mitchell, an elementary school teacher who had moved to town last year. Caitlin waved her friend over. She liked Mary Beth. The two of them had hit it off since the first day Mary Beth had agreed to deliver hot meals now and then for Good Neighbors.

As the young woman crossed the street, an idea took shape in Caitlin's mind. Why hadn't she thought of this before? Mary Beth was exactly the sort of person Brent was looking for. She was smart, fun, and attractive, with light auburn hair and pretty green eyes. Most importantly, Mary Beth wanted to live in

Desmond; and, based on her enthusiasm for her class, she loved children.

That had been her error last night. Caitlin had thought going out with Mason would make her forget about Brent. Instead, she needed to get Brent to go out with another woman. Caitlin smiled. It was so simple. If Brent were involved with someone else . . . Well, then, she certainly wouldn't be attracted to him. She wasn't that type. He'd be off-limits, and she could stop wanting him.

And Mary Beth was absolutely perfect for Brent. Caitlin pushed away the faint uneasiness that passed through her at the thought. Instead, she forced herself to concentrate on the positives. Brent deserved this. He was a special man, a kind, considerate . . . unbelievably sexy man. Whoops. Caitlin yanked her thoughts back in line. Where was she? Oh, right. He was a great guy who deserved someone sweet like Mary Beth.

"How have you been?" Mary Beth stopped next to her, smiling.

"Good. You know, I've been meaning to call you." Caitlin debated how to broach the subject of Brent. She tried to never fix up her friends, but this plan was too perfect for words. It was guaranteed not to fail, and she was proud of herself for thinking it up.

"I've been meaning to call you, too," Mary Beth said. "I want a chance to visit before you move. I know, why don't you come to dinner tonight?"

Her friend had unwittingly given her the exact opening she needed. Struggling to remain calm, Caitlin said, "That sounds like fun. But would you mind if I brought someone with me? Brent Stewart is taking over Good Neighbors for me when I leave. Since you volunteer for us, I'd know he'd like to meet you. And he could come over with me, since he lives right next door to my apartment."

Darn it. She was babbling and sounding overly anxious. Mary Beth would probably turn her down flat. As she waited for her friend to responsd, she pushed away the annoying emotions that beset her at the thought of fixing Brent up. Maybe Mary Beth wouldn't even like Brent. Maybe she'd positively detest him.

Mary Beth's wide smile squashed those concerns. "Brent Stewart? The new cop?"

Caitlin recognized this look. She'd seen it on many female faces ever since she'd been a kid. It was that eat-him-up-with-a-spoon look women got when they talked about Brent. "Have you met him?"

"Met him, no. Seen him, yes." Mary Beth leaned toward Caitlin and said quietly, "He's gorgeous. I'd be thrilled to meet him."

An uncomfortable queasiness settled in Caitlin's stomach. Mary Beth was just like all the other women in town. The schoolteacher wasn't immune to Brent's good looks. And unlike some handsome guys, Brent was also trustworthy. Clean-cut. Honorable. Mary Beth wouldn't find anyone better.

Caitlin forced herself to smile. "Great. What time should we come over?"

Mary Beth's smile was nothing short of radiant, and Caitlin wanted to kick herself. Now she definitely needed to stop kissing Brent. Her friend had already fallen under his spell, and she hadn't even met him yet. And since Mary Beth was a sweet person, Brent would really like her, too. Brent was looking for a great woman to settle down with, and Caitlin had found him one.

Peachy keen. Wasn't this working out wonderfully for everyone concerned? Arrgh. What was wrong with her? She should be happy about this. This was precisely what she wanted.

But she knew what was wrong with her, and it scared her clear down to her toenails. She was jealous—of Mary Beth!—the very woman who was going to make her plan succeed.

Yep, there was no doubt about it any longer, Caitlin decided. She had officially lost her mind.

"You've set me up with a blind date?" Brent stood in the driveway to his house, staring at Caitlin. He'd just started washing his car when she'd walked over, looking amazingly sexy in her blue shorts and pale blue T-shirt. He turned off the water to the hose and stared at her. "Why would you do something like that?"

"It's not a blind date." She leaned over to look in the bucket. "Where's the sponge? I'll help wash your car."

From this angle, Brent had a really nice view of the swell of Caitlin's breasts. Dear Lord. He moved away from her, feeling like a jerk. Did she have any idea what she was doing to him? Granted, women all over town wore shorts and T-shirts during the summer. And there was nothing in the least risqué about her outfit. He could easily tell she was wearing a bra, and not even one of the new kinds that gave women incredible cleavage. No, Caitlin was more than decent, but he couldn't remember the last time he'd been so turned on.

He cleared his suddenly dry throat and tried to

think straight. What had they been talking about? Oh, yeah. The blind date. "I don't want to go."

Caitlin was washing the hood of his Suburban. She tipped her head, brushing back the hair from the side of her face so she could look at him. "Why not? Mary Beth's sweet and she's very pretty. She's also exactly what you're looking for—someone who wants to live in Desmond and have a family." She smiled, but that smile didn't reach her deep blue eyes. Interesting. Apparently, Caitlin wasn't too thrilled about the idea of this date. Then why had she set him up?

"If it helps, Mary Beth did mention that she thinks you're gorgeous," Caitlin added.

Brent didn't know whether to be angry or insulted. The only thing he knew for certain was that he wasn't flattered. "You discussed me with this woman?"

Caitlin blinked at him, obviously surprised by his stern tone. "I didn't really discuss you. She invited me to dinner, and I asked if I could bring you along. Mary Beth knows who you are, although you probably haven't been back in town long enough to meet her."

"So your friend asked you to dinner, and you decided to use it as an opportunity to fix me up?" He was truly stunned she'd done this. Oh sure, last night they'd decided not to kiss anymore, but that didn't mean he wanted Caitlin to find dates for him. She had to have a reason for doing this. "You're up to something."

Caitlin came over to stand in front of him. "No, I'm not. Mary Beth volunteers for Good Neighbors. I thought you might want to meet her, so when she asked me to dinner, bringing you along seemed the logical thing to do. I know you're really going to like her."

Her plan became clear to Brent, and anger rushed through him in a torrent. This really bothered him. "You think I'm going to fall for your friend, and then you'll be safe, right?"

She hesitated, then said, "It's not like that."

He dropped the hose and lightly put one hand on her arm. Beneath his fingers, he could feel her warm skin and his body stirred with awareness again. "So tell me what it is like."

"It's nothing but a simple dinner. That's all. No one expects you to fall in love with Mary Beth."

"But you are hoping it'll cool things off. Between you and me, I mean. Your date with Gibbs didn't work out and you figure it's my turn."

For countless tense moments, they stared at each other, and all Brent could think about was how much he wanted to kiss her, right here, right now. In the middle of the driveway to his house. In plain view of anyone passing by. The gleam in her eyes showed him clearly that she felt the same desire. Her pupils dilated, and her gaze dropped to his lips. She wanted to kiss him, too. But it wasn't going to happen.

"You drive me crazy, Caitlin," he said with a sigh. Then, reluctantly, he removed his hand from her arm and moved away from her. This whole situation was getting out of hand. Maybe she was right. Maybe if he fell for someone else, he could stop thinking about Caitlin.

Brent picked up the sponge she'd dropped and returned to washing his car. Behind him, he could almost hear her thinking. Planning. Scheming. Eventually, she turned and headed back to her apartment.

"I take it you accept the invitation," she said over her shoulder as she walked away.

"I wouldn't miss this dinner for the world," he muttered, watching her walk away from him.

Brent was being incredibly charming, and it was ticking Caitlin off. All through dinner, he'd been witty and sweet and just plain wonderful. She couldn't remember the last time she'd been this annoyed.

Mary Beth obviously thought Brent had hung the moon, and now the two of them were in the kitchen together doing the dishes. Caitlin had offered to help, but her friend assured her the two of them could handle things.

As he'd followed Mary Beth into the kitchen, Brent had given Caitlin a look that had made her want to either slap him or kiss him so hard his ancestors felt it.

She was jealous, and she knew it. She hated the fact that she could be so petty, but it was a fact. And she didn't know what to do about her feelings. They were stupid anyway. Brent was wrong for her. He was right for Mary Beth. Simple as that. Plus, she was their friend. She should be happy for them.

So why couldn't she help hoping that there'd be no chemistry whatsoever between Brent and Mary Beth? No zing. No zip. No zap.

Nothing.

"Because I'm a terrible person," she muttered to herself. They both seemed to be having a terrific time, and she was miserable. It was obvious Mary Beth was attracted to Brent. But how did he feel?

That question was driving her crazy.

With a soft groan, she stood and paced the small living room, trying to ignore the laughter coming from the kitchen. This was a good thing, dammit. A great thing. If Brent started dating Mary Beth, then Caitlin would have to leave him alone. She'd have to stop thinking about kissing him and touching him and doing a lot of other things with him.

She'd finally be able to concentrate on her upcoming move to Dallas.

When Mary Beth giggled again, Caitlin clenched her fists. She h-a-t-e-d this.

For almost ten more minutes, she endured it. With determination, she paced and tried to tune out the happy sounds coming from the other room. When the cell phone in her purse rang, Caitlin grabbed it like a drowning woman lunging for a life preserver.

It was her father. "Hey, Caity, honey, is Brent with you by any chance?"

Caitlin glanced toward the kitchen. Was Brent with her? Well, sort of. To her father, she said, "Yes. He's here. What's up?"

"A young woman named Alice Hirsch just called. She's alone except for her small son, and she's gone into labor. The ambulance is out on a call, and all my officers are busy. I thought Brent might swing by and get her to the hospital. Oh, and her son's going to need someone to take care of him. I thought Good Neighbors could help with that."

Caitlin's instincts took over. "We're on our way."

When she walked into the kitchen, Brent and Mary Beth turned to look at her. Caitlin quickly explained the problem, and the awkward evening came to a merciful end. Mary Beth walked them out to Brent's Suburban. Caitlin got in and waited while Brent finished talking to the other woman. As each second ticked by, she became increasingly impatient. What was taking so long?

She was about to remind Brent of the urgency of the situation when a new, and unbearably disturbing thought occurred to her. Was Brent kissing Mary Beth good-bye? Caitlin's heart sank at the thought. It was dark outside, and she couldn't see much through the driver's side windows.

Suddenly Brent opened his door and climbed inside.

"Ready to go?" he asked, starting the car.

Caitlin felt her nervous tension slowly ease. "You have no idea."

"Nice dinner," Brent said as he backed down Mary Beth's driveway. "Do you have directions to this house?"

Caitlin hadn't looked at him yet or said a word since he'd gotten in the car. She quickly told him how to get to the house and what she knew about Alice Hirsch and her son.

Then she fell silent again.

He glanced briefly at her, wondering what she was thinking. She sat perfectly straight, her gaze fixed on the road ahead of them. A light rain started to fall, and Brent welcomed the distraction. He turned on the windshield wipers.

Finally, the silence got to Brent. "Do you know someone who can take care of her son while she's in the hospital?"

"I can call Reverend Williams and his wife. They probably can."

Silence invaded the car again. When they were

almost to Alice Hirsch's house, Brent had had enough. "Mind telling me what the problem is?"

"There's no problem."

He laughed ruefully. "Oh. Right. You're just ignoring me because you think I like it."

"I'm not ignoring you. I'm worried about this woman."

He might have believed her except he knew Caitlin chattered when she was nervous or upset. She clammed up when she was angry.

There was no doubt she was angry right now.

"You fixed me up with your friend, Caitlin. So what do you have to be angry about?" He kept his tone even, but it wasn't easy, considering his frustration. The woman he wanted was the wrong one for him, and in an attempt to avoid what was happening between them, she'd fixed him up with her friend.

"I'm not angry." She spoke each word slowly, distinctly. Then with a sigh, she said, "I think I'm jealous."

Jealous? She was jealous? Brent couldn't help it. He smiled. "Really?"

"Yes, but it makes me mad at myself that I am, so stop smiling. The truth is, I can't stand the idea of you being with Mary Beth." She groaned. "I know, I'm being irrational."

Brent chuckled, feeling oddly cheered by her admission. But she sounded so miserable that he took pity on her. "Well, I was jealous last night. Guess we're even."

"But you had no reason to be jealous of Mason. He's a jerk. Mary Beth is a really nice woman. She's perfect for you."

Brent turned his Suburban into the driveway of a

small, white house on the edge of town. As he pulled up next to the house, he said, "I know she's nice. I had a good time with her tonight." Switching off the engine, he turned toward Caitlin. "The only thing wrong with Mary Beth is that she isn't you. And whether I like it or not, I seem to be fixated on you at the moment."

He wasn't certain what reaction he expected from Caitlin, but the only response he got was a subdued "Oh."

When it became obvious she wasn't going to say anything else, he pushed open his car door and climbed out. Then he headed to her side of the car, but before he got there, Caitlin climbed out and headed toward the porch steps. He followed, wondering what she was thinking.

When they reached the front door, she said without looking at him, "Me, too. I mean, I'm fixated. On you."

There were countless things Brent wanted to say to her, but instead, he knocked on the door. A little boy about five opened the door, tears streaming down his face.

Brent identified himself and Caitlin, then asked, "What's your name?"

"Peter Hirsch."

"And where's your mother?"

The boy hiccupped around a sob. "Mommy's sick in bed."

Caitlin led Peter into the living room and spoke to him softly while Brent went down the narrow hall until he found Alice Hirsch. Rather than resting, she was sitting on the side of the bed, breathing loudly.

Brent's training kicked in. "Mrs. Hirsch, I'm Officer Brent Stewart of the Desmond Police. I'm here to get you to the hospital."

Alice nodded. "Thanks. What about Peter? Is he okay?"

"Caitlin Rogers, the head of our local volunteer organization, is going to make certain Peter is taken care of. We need to get you to the hospital. Is there anyone we should notify?"

She shook her head. "No. No one. My husband died almost eight months ago. It's just me and Peter now."

Wanting to keep her focused on the present, Brent said, "And the little one who seems to be about to join your family."

Alice gave him a wan smile. "Yes. And the baby."

Working together, Brent and Caitlin quickly got Alice and Peter in the car and headed toward the hospital. Caitlin had had the foresight to retrieve Peter's favorite toys for the ride. And since her son was now calm, Alice could focus on her contractions, which were closer together with every passing minute.

Thankfully, the hospital wasn't far away. Brent pulled up in front and dropped off Alice and Caitlin, then he went with Peter to find a parking space. It took a while, but finally they parked. He could tell the little boy was trying to be tough, but it had to be hard.

As they walked toward the hospital, Brent said, "Are you looking forward to being a big brother?"

Peter shook his head. "No."

Well, that was honest enough. "Why not?"

"What if Mommy likes the baby better?"

Brent stopped and studied the kid. Peter looked so worried, it tugged at Brent's heart. He wasn't really the right one to tell a child about a mother's love. His mother hadn't loved him. She'd dumped him at his grandmother's and had never looked back. But Peter's mother obviously wasn't like Brent's mother. Not at all. Knowing he was telling the truth, he knelt in front of Peter and assured him, "That won't happen. Your mom will love you just as much after the baby arrives as she did before."

"You sure?"

"Positive," Brent said, his heart breaking for the little guy. It had to be tough. His dad dead, his mom in the hospital. Brent stood and headed back toward the hospital. "Let's go see if anyone needs our help."

Peter nodded. "Okay."

And Brent knew in that second how desperately he wanted to be a father. He'd made the right choice coming back to Desmond. He would find the right woman and settle down.

An image of Caitlin floated across his brain, but he ignored it. Caitlin wouldn't be the woman. No, when he got married, it would be to someone else. Someone different but also special.

Just not Caitlin.

Caitlin looked up as Brent and Peter entered the waiting room. They were talking in hushed, intense voices and after giving her a brief smile, Brent led Peter over to a table where crayons and coloring books were scattered about.

Once Peter was coloring, Brent glanced at Caitlin, his gaze so direct it made her heart beat faster.

"Alice okay?"

Caitlin nodded. "The nurse said the baby should be born soon. Alice is really far along."

Peter looked up at her words. "Is Mommy okay?"

She could clearly hear the fear in his voice. "Yes. She's fine."

Peter turned to Brent, apparently for confirmation. Brent smiled and nodded. "Yeah, she's fine. And soon you're going to be a big brother. It's going to be a lot more fun than you think. For starters, you'll no longer be the baby of the family. Your mom will know you're a big guy now."

"I guess." Peter studied the picture he was coloring. When he glanced back at Brent, the tears were gone from his eyes. "Are you sure my mommy knows I'm the big brother? Maybe you should tell her."

Rather than laugh at the child's question, Brent appeared to give it serious thought. "I'm sure she knows, but if you want me to check on that, I will."

Peter nodded. "You should. And tell her that other stuff, too. About the love."

Curious, Caitlin looked at Brent. "What stuff about love?"

Peter answered before Brent could. "He said Mommy will love me as much after the baby is born as she did before."

Caitlin's throat tightened. She looked at Brent, but his attention was focused on Peter. "Officer Stewart is right. Your mom told me how much she loves you while we were checking in. She's very proud of you, too."

Which she was. Alice Hirsch had said wonderful things about her son. Caitlin knew without a doubt that she would love both of her children equally.

Almost as if he sensed her gaze, Brent turned his

head and looked at her. Caitlin felt the impact of that look clear to her toes, and a sudden realization hit her.

She was falling in love with Brent. Oh, no. What in the world was she supposed to do now?

Chapter Six

Being attracted to Brent was bad enough, but falling in love? Caitlin couldn't believe she'd been so foolish.

Well, she would just have to unfall right back out of love. That was the only solution. She didn't want to get to Dallas dragging a broken heart with her, and that was the only way this threepenny circus could end.

While she was lost in thought, a nurse appeared at the entrance to the waiting room. She looked at Caitlin and Brent. "Mrs. Hirsch had a girl. She and the baby are doing fine and will be transferred to their room in a few minutes." Glancing at Peter, she added, "Your mom wants to see you."

After the nurse left, Brent helped Peter finish his drawing so he could give it to Alice. As Caitlin watched Brent work with the small boy, she knew she had her work cut out for her. Unfalling in love with Brent Stewart was going to be next to impossible.

But she had to try. She had to try really hard.

"Now remember," Brent said to Peter. "Your mother and sister are very tired. They need to get some sleep, so we'll only stay a short time."

Peter nodded, then slipped his small hand into Brent's. With a smile, Brent held Peter's hand and they walked to the hospital room. Caitlin walked next to them, and was oddly silent. This time, Brent knew her silence wasn't due to anger. No, something else was bothering Caitlin.

He would have to ask her about that later, but right now, he wanted to help Peter.

Pushing open the door to the room, he waited while Peter peeked inside. When the boy saw his mother, he ran to her bedside. Although she was utterly exhausted, Alice gathered her son into the bed with her, making certain he was careful around the baby in her arms.

"This is your new sister. What do you think?"

Peter looked at the small bundle, then shrugged. "She's kinda funny-looking, but I guess she's okay."

Brent walked over to the bed and looked at the baby. In his opinion, the newborn was beautiful. He looked at Caitlin, who still stood several feet away, almost as if she didn't want to get too close to the family scene.

"What are you going to call her?" Brent asked.

Peter looked at him and wrinkled his nose. "Mommy says I can call her Katie."

"But her real name is Katherine," Alice said, smiling at her son. Then she looked at Brent. "I can't thank you enough for driving me here. I didn't know what to do. My sister is coming in a couple of weeks to help with Peter and the baby, but she can't come sooner. Until she gets here, I'm on my own. I hate to ask, but you said something about knowing someone Peter could stay with."

Caitlin moved forward. "I've spoken to Reverend Williams. He and his wife said they'd be thrilled to take care of Peter for a few days. Brent or I would keep him with us, but since we both work, we figured the reverend and his wife would be a better choice."

"I've met him before," Alice said. "Peter and I went to Sunday services a few times when we first moved here."

Peter looked at Brent. "Can't I stay with you?"

Knowing the boy was nervous, Brent patted his shoulder. "No, because I'm working a morning shift tomorrow. But I'll come over after I finish work and we can play."

Rather than argue, Peter accepted his answer. "Okay. If you promise."

His comment made Brent smile. He was glad Peter liked him. He liked the little boy, too. "I promise."

Peter kissed his mother's cheek, and after only a brief hesitation, kissed his newborn sister's forehead. Then they left and headed to the parking lot. Peter was walking so slowly long before they reached the car that Brent picked him up and carried him the rest of the way. When they got to the Suburban, he buckled the now-sleeping boy into the backseat.

"Heck of a night," Brent said after Caitlin was seated and they headed back toward town.

"Isn't that the truth."

"See, you didn't have to go all the way to Dallas to have an exciting evening. Things got pretty wild here," he teased.

Caitlin laughed softly. "It was almost too exciting for me."

He could still sense her tension. Was she upset about admitting that she was jealous of Mary Beth or was there something else? Whatever was bothering her, he got the feeling she wasn't going to discuss it with him right now.

Instead of pushing her, he said, "The Hirsch kids are cute, aren't they? Peter's a great kid, and despite what he said, his new baby sister is adorable."

"Um. I guess."

When it became apparent that was all she was going to say on the subject, Brent let it go. What had he expected? That seeing a couple of cute kids would somehow change Caitlin's mind? That suddenly she'd decide she wanted to stay in Desmond and raise a family . . . with him?

Talk about wishful thinking. Caitlin had her life planned, and she deserved her dreams. But for him, tonight only reinforced his desire to have children. He'd really had fun with Peter, and he was now positive he wanted kids of his own.

He let the silence in the car remain unbroken as he drove to Reverend Williams's house to drop off Peter. After they got the boy settled, he drove back to his house and parked in the garage. Tonight, there was no repeat of the searing kiss of last night. Instead, Caitlin got out of the car almost the second he turned off the engine. He caught up with her as she was crossing over to her apartment.

"Thanks for everything," she said, still walking.

Brent easily kept pace with her. "That's it? We're not going to talk about any of this?"

Caitlin stopped and turned to face him. She looked weary. "Can we let everything go for right now? I need to get some rest. Like you said, it was a pretty exciting night."

Brent didn't want to drop the subject. But he had no right to press her. Maybe she was right. Maybe now wasn't the right time to thrash this out.

"Sure. We'll let it go for right now," he said.

She gave him a small smile. "Thanks. I'll see you in the morning."

Brent nodded and watched her walk up the stairs to her apartment. He was tired, too, and had no idea what he and Caitlin should do about their situation.

Two days later, Caitlin got ready to go to the hospital with Brent to pick up Alice. She decided she'd done such a good job avoiding the man for the last few days that she could teach spies how to skulk. She'd developed almost a sixth sense when it came to him. And it wasn't easy avoiding a man who lived right next door to you and worked for your father. Not to mention a man she was supposed to be training to take over her volunteer work. But she'd managed it. Their only contact had been one short phone call during which she'd explained they were short of help at the moment and given him some tasks to do.

Then she'd taken her own to-do list and headed out—in the opposite direction. She wasn't trying to be mean to him, she simply needed time to think. Lots and lots of time to think.

After examining her feelings closely, she'd come

to the conclusion she wasn't in love with Brent at all. She was in lust. Overwhelmingly so. Mixed in with that purely physical feeling was a healthy dose of admiration. No wonder she'd mistaken what she was feeling for love. It couldn't possibly be love, though.

And it certainly wasn't an emotion that could in any way change her plans to move to Dallas. Feeling much better about everything, Caitlin locked her apartment and headed down the stairs. She could see Brent was already loading things into his Suburban. Putting a smile on her face, she walked across the lawn to his driveway.

When he stopped what he was doing and looked at her, Caitlin's heart did a little thumpity-thump-thump, which she ignored.

"Lust," she muttered to herself. "Pure lust. That's all."

Brent looked confused. "What did you say?"

"Nothing." She moved to the back of the car. Today they were taking Peter to pick up his mother and newborn sister from the hospital. Glancing inside the Suburban, Caitlin saw a crib still in the box. Intrigued, she peeked into a couple of the bags Brent had loaded, ignoring his protests. They were filled with clothes and toys for both Peter and the baby.

Ah, he wasn't making this not-being-in-love stuff easy. When she turned to ask him about the presents, he looked downright embarrassed. And cute enough to kiss.

Arrgh! She wasn't going to.

"Seems you ran into a big sale somewhere," she said.

Brent sighed. "Okay, I bought them a few things. Not much. I noticed when I was at their house yesterday that they don't have much. Katie doesn't even have a crib to sleep in.''

"Why were you at their house yesterday? It wasn't on your Good Neighbors run."

Brent picked up another bag off the driveway and put it in the car. Caitlin noticed it was filled with diapers. "When Peter and I stopped by the hospital to visit Alice, she asked if I could go to the house and pick up a couple of things for her."

"So while you were there, you noticed they didn't have much and decided to help out."

Brent turned to face her. "Yes. Okay. I did. Is there some Good Neighbors rule that says I can't?"

Caitlin smiled. Although by being such a good guy, Brent was making it difficult for her to resist him, he also was proving her right. Brent was perfect for this job.

"I think it's great. But you didn't have to buy everything. Lots of the local merchants will donate things if you ask them. Plus we have a fund for occasions like this."

"Peter said his mother won't take charity."

Caitlin leaned over and picked up another bag. It contained canned goods. Brent certainly was looking out for the Hirsch family.

"I'm not suggesting charity. But Alice needs help, and there are organizations and people out there to help her," she said.

Brent placed his hand on her arm, the look in his deep brown eyes intense. "I'm one of those people, Caitlin. I did this because I wanted to do it. Just like you do all the thousands of things you do. Don't make a big deal out of it."

Standing this close, he seemed to surround her

senses. His eyes darkened even more as he looked at her. And as the seconds ticked by, the mood between them shifted . . . became charged with awareness. With desire. Caitlin clenched her fists by her side. He looked so sexy standing there in his jeans and T-shirt, so male and handsome that she wanted to—

She told herself again that all she was feeling was lust. So what if he'd bought toys for a widow and her two small children? So what if he climbed up on a roof to help an elderly couple? All she felt for Brent was lust. And if she exercised a little willpower, she could gain control over this situation.

She glanced back at Brent. The look he gave her was nothing short of smoldering. It heated her blood and made her fantasize about sultry nights and satin sheets and whispered words. She tried to hold on to logic, hang on to reason, but her willpower was nowhere to be seen. All she could focus on was Brent and how irresistible he looked at this moment.

Oh, no.

Without hesitation, she leaned up and kissed him. Hard.

Brent hadn't seen the kiss coming, wasn't even sure why she was kissing him, but now that Caitlin was in his arms, he did what any red-blooded man would do—he took advantage of the situation.

Aligning her body against his so she could feel just how much he wanted her, he took a sensual pleasure in her unexpected kiss. He was hot for her. He'd missed seeing her, being with her the last couple of days. Caitlin was quickly becoming very important to him. Maybe too important.

But at the moment, he didn't care if he was condemning himself to a broken heart. He was tired of pretending he didn't want her, didn't need her. So he let her know how he felt, with his passionate response, with his roving hands. He caressed her body, and courted her heart.

Caitlin didn't resist any of his overtures. When he slipped his tongue into her mouth, she met him eagerly with her own. Tasting each other. Needing each other. When he slipped his right hand down from her shoulder and cupped one firm breast, she didn't pull back. Rather, she leaned into the caress, moaning softly when he found her hard nipple and rubbed it with his thumb.

Desire had become all. His blood thrummed through his body, his senses overwhelmed by the nearness of Caitlin. He desperately wanted to make love to her, to show her what she meant to him. But this certainly wasn't the place, and now certainly wasn't the time. Reluctantly, he took his hands away from her tempting body, and by slow degrees, he broke the kiss.

He gazed into her eyes, seeing the need in them. But then she blinked and looked away. He wanted to say something to her, anything, but rational thought escaped him. He was still too shaken by the kiss . . . that had been so very much more. It had shaken him to the core, and he had no idea what to do now.

Caitlin seemed equally confused. Silently, they loaded the rest of the groceries into the car and headed to the reverend's house to collect Peter.

Peter looked down at his sleeping sister, then glanced back up at Caitlin.

"She's kinda wrinkly," he said solemnly.

Caitlin smiled. "No, Katie's not. She's just a little baby, and that's what they look like." To tell the truth, Katie was adorable, and just looking at her was doing all sorts of weird things to Caitlin's emotions. She stepped back from the crib, not waiting to think about biological clocks and maternal drives now. Especially not right now. Not when Brent's kiss was still making her melt inside.

"Let's leave Katie to sleep and go look at all those great toys Brent brought you," Caitlin said, heading toward the bedroom door with Peter trailing behind her. When they reached the living room, she took a deep breath, wanting to clear her lungs of the sweet baby smell.

Yet still the scent lingered. The smell of new life. New hope. Caitlin glanced at Brent, who having assembled the crib in time for Katie's nap, was now wrestling with a couple of Peter's toys, trying to get them together too.

Almost as if he sensed her gaze, Brent looked at her. For a heartbeat, she lost herself in his deep, brown gaze. Would his babies all have those same gorgeous eyes? Or would they—

Yikes. Double yikes. Caitlin deliberately looked away. Someone should put those plastic yellow caution signs around the man. Babies? What in the world was she doing thinking about babies? A few years from now she could think about things like that, but not now. Not now.

She needed to get that through her head. It was one thing to have lustful fantasies about the man, but she drew the line at visions of motherhood.

Brent finished putting together an action figure, which Peter snagged out of his hands with a whoop of joy and a hasty thank-you. Brent chuckled and picked up his tools.

"Guess he likes the toys," he said.

"I can't tell you how much we appreciate everything you've done for us," Alice told them.

Caitlin smiled, glad to have something else to focus on rather than her confusing feelings for Brent. "It's been our pleasure. And there's still a lot more Good Neighbors is going to do. You have the list of folks who will be stopping by with food and to give you a break, right?"

"Yes." Alice moved forward and gave Caitlin a hug. Then she hugged Brent. "You're both so special. This would have been so difficult without your help."

"We're just glad we could be there for you," Brent said.

And Caitlin knew he meant it. As she'd worked with him, she'd come to realize he liked helping out as much as she did. It made her feel good to know that Good Neighbors would be in such capable hands after she left.

The thought of leaving suddenly filled her with a touch of sadness rather than the usual exhilaration. Which was silly. She wanted to go to Dallas. She wanted to start her new job. The only explanation she had for her mixed emotions was that she was reluctant to leave Brent for some reason. But after all, she was as human as the next woman. His kisses kept stirring her up with no release. Desire made her edgy, jumpy. And confused about a lot of things.

She glanced at Brent again, who was saying goodbye to Peter. If unresolved lust was her problem, then the solution was obvious—she simply had to make love with Brent. They needed to deal directly with this physical attraction. Get it out of their systems. Then she could leave town with no regrets.

Caitlin smiled, liking her idea more and more. Life would be simple again. She was sure he would cooperate.

Caitlin was acting weird, that much Brent knew. He just didn't know why. But ever since they'd left the Hirsch family, she kept smiling at him. Not normal smiles. But flirty smiles. Sexy smiles that were upsetting his equilibrium.

She had to know what she was doing. Caitlin was a smart woman. So why would she want to get him revved up? She was the one who wanted to leave town. Getting involved certainly didn't fit into her plans.

"I don't have to be back to town anytime soon. Why don't we swing by that land your grandmother left you up at Turner Lake?" she asked, her voice oh-so-sweet. "You and my brothers still use the cabin when you go fishing there, right?"

That was it. Brent pulled the Suburban off to the side of the road and turned to face her. "What's up?"

The siren's smile on her face didn't disappear. "I don't know what you mean."

Brent forced himself to stay focused. "You do too know what I mean. I thought you'd be upset about that kiss back at my house this morning. Instead, you're—" He waved one hand at her, at a loss for words. Finally, he said, "You're flirting with me. And asking me to drive you to Turner Lake. And asking about the cabin. Why do you want to go there?"

Caitlin laughed, the soft sound arousing all his

senses. "Now, Brent, why do you think I want to go there?"

Lots of reasons came to mind, all of which were exciting. "Why don't you tell me?"

She glanced around. They were still parked on the shoulder of the two-lane back road. "Do you want to talk about it here? Wouldn't we be more comfortable at the cabin?"

Brent wanted to get comfortable at the cabin, all right, but he cared too much about Caitlin not to level with her. "If we go to the cabin, I'm afraid I may not be able to resist kissing you."

Her smile widened. "Oh, goody."

She wasn't making this easy. He pressed on, needing her to understand. "Caitlin, I probably won't be able to stop at kisses. I can't keep doing this. I want you, Caitlin. You know that. If we go there, something may happen."

This time, her smile became a grin. "Oh, double goody."

Brent was fairly certain his heart stopped beating for a second. "What?"

"Take me to the cabin, Brent," she said in a sultry voice. "The only way we're going to get this out of our systems is to do something."

"I'm not sure that's a good idea," he started, but when a large truck went by them, coming too close for comfort, Brent decided she was right about one thing. The side of the road wasn't the place to have this conversation. But as far as he was concerned, he hadn't agreed to anything yet.

Without comment, he drove a few more miles to Turner Lake. In addition to the house in Desmond, his grandmother had left him this land, a little over twenty acres, with a clear, cool lake in the middle of it and a small cabin he and the Rogers brothers used when they went fishing. Brent had lots of great memories of this place. Each summer, he and the Rogers kids and Dan had come here to go fishing, swimming, and have campouts. Since moving back to Desmond, he, Tony, and Al had come here a couple of times, cleaned up the cabin and stocked it again for future visits.

All of which Caitlin undoubtedly knew. Silently, he pulled his Suburban in front of the cabin and turned off the engine. He'd always liked this place, probably because he had created lasting memories at this cabin. He glanced at Caitlin. It looked like he was about to make another great memory.

"Remember when we used to come here to go swimming?" Caitlin asked, almost as if she were reading his mind. "Then we'd fish for dinner. I loved those trips. Marshmallows and ghost stories around the fire. Then Dad would put sleeping bags out on the cabin floor, but I don't think we ever slept more than two hours. You and my brothers would never shut up."

Brent chuckled and turned to look at her. "Us? You were the motormouth. Always telling the scariest stories."

"It was fun." She glanced around, then unhooked her seat belt and shifted in her seat so she was facing him. "Did you ever bring girlfriends here? You know, to make out . . . and stuff."

He'd thought about it, but he hadn't. "No," he admitted. "So are you really sure about this?"

"Yes. If you're interested."

Interested? Hell, yes. But he still had one important question.

"Why? You're the one who keeps saying that since you're leaving we shouldn't get involved. I can't imagine getting much more involved than making love."

Caitlin reached down and yanked her T-shirt free of her jeans. Brent's heart slammed against his ribs and his breath stuck in his throat. Damn. If her hands hadn't trembled just the slightest bit, he might be tempted to believe she really was ready for this. But she wasn't. Not at all.

"It's become almost impossible for us to work together. We're friends, Brent. We've been friends practically forever. We can't let all these feelings and whatnot get in the way. So my idea is to just do it. Then things can get back to normal."

"You don't seriously believe that, do you? If we make love, Caitlin, it will change everything."

Her gaze was serious as it met his. "No, it won't. We won't let it. And we both know this isn't about forever. It's about right now. I'm still moving to Dallas at the end of the month. And you're still staying right here in Desmond. But you're driving me crazy." She tipped her head and the look she gave him was sizzling. "Am I driving you crazy, too?"

Apparently, because he was going to agree to this. "Hell, yes, Caitlin. All I think about is you."

"Brent, our being together—here—is the right thing to do. It will simplify everything."

He laughed without humor. She couldn't be serious. "Caitlin, I can't resist you anymore. That's the only reason I'm agreeing. I want you, more than anything. But I'm not foolish enough to think making love with you will make my life simple. I know it won't."

"Let's find out."

Before he could change his mind, he threw open his door, walked to the back of his car, and got out the blankets he carried in the back in case of an emergency. Then he walked to the cabin and unlocked it. He knew Caitlin was watching him, but she didn't say anything. Instead, she climbed out of the car and walked over to stand next to him. Her smile told him she knew she'd convinced him.

"You're sure, right?" he asked, giving her one last chance to change her mind.

She grinned, looking unbelievably happy. "Yes, yes, yes. You?"

"Yeah, I'm sure. I'm insane, but I'm sure."

He waved her inside the cabin. "After you," he said, praying she really was as sure as she claimed she was. And hoping he could do this and not end up spending the rest of his live missing Caitlin after she left.

But he really didn't have much choice anymore because Caitlin had already walked inside the cabin. As he watched, she pulled her T-shirt over her head. He took one look at her blue lace bra and knew he was hers for as long as she wanted him.

Sealing his own fate, he walked inside the cabin and shut the door.

Chapter Seven

Caitlin wasn't the slightest bit embarrassed or uncomfortable with Brent once he closed the door. All she felt was excitement. Pure excitement. Being with Brent was the right thing to do. She was certain of it. Thank goodness he agreed. She couldn't take much more of the push-pull between them.

"I feel like I'm sixteen years old, doing this in the old cabin," Brent said, opening the blankets and spreading them in front of the fireplace. He waited until Caitlin sat on the blankets, then he stretched out next to her, his tall frame almost filling the small area.

Caitlin lay down beside him, then leaned forward and trailed a stream of kisses along his jaw. "Want me to go slow and pretend this is your first time?"

Brent chuckled. "No, thanks." Reaching over behind her, he flicked open her bra, removing it like a pro. "I don't think I can go slow. I feel like I've wanted you forever."

Caitlin felt the same way, and when he cupped her face, she gave herself over to the joy of his kiss. While he leaned over her, exploring her mouth, she wrapped her fingers around one of his hands and slowly moved it down until it rested on her right breast.

If her action surprised him, he didn't show it. Not even when she pressed into his palm. As soon as he cupped her weight, a sigh slipped from her lips, the quiet sound quickly captured by his mouth. Slowly, with infinite care, he fondled her, his fingers finding and coaxing her nipple into a tight bud. Caitlin felt desire tighten within her, finally settling between her legs.

With a groan, he tore his mouth away from hers and looked down at her bare breasts.

"You are so pretty," he said, seconds before dipping his head and taking one nipple into his mouth. He suckled the sensitive tip until Caitlin writhed beneath him. Then he moved to her other breast.

Caitlin had never felt such ecstasy, never cared for a man as she did for Brent. She reached for him, wanting to feel his flesh, wanting to touch him and make him feel the pleasure he was giving her.

Grasping the cotton of his T-shirt, she tugged. "You have on way too many clothes," she complained.

Brent chuckled, leaning up and pulling his T-shirt off with one fluid motion. "Happy now?"

More like speechless. Brent's body had always been impressive. As a teen, she'd often seen him without his shirt, swimming with her brothers, working on a construction project. She'd dreamed of touching his chest.

And here was her chance. She reached out and trailed her fingers over his well-defined muscles, stopping when she noticed a scar on the side of his waist.

"What happened?" she asked, moving closer to get a better look. She didn't really need to ask what had caused the scar. Instinctively, she knew.

"You were shot, weren't you?" she asked, fear skittering through her at the thought of Brent being shot. "This happened in Dallas, didn't it?"

He shrugged off her concern. "It wasn't such a big deal, Caitlin."

How could he say that?

"You were shot. That's a big deal."

Brent reached out and cupped her breasts in his hands. "No offense, but that's the last thing on my mind right now."

Although, he might not want to talk about it at this moment, she wasn't about to let the subject drop. Of course, when he thumbed her taut nipples, she had a hard time remembering what it was she wanted to talk to him about, and when he pulled her close and she felt the hard length of his arousal, she had a hard time remembering anything at all.

They quickly shed what was left of their clothing. For many long minutes, the only sounds filling the small cabin were murmurs and moans. Caitlin took her time learning what aroused Brent most, exploring his body with boldness. When he insisted on being given equal liberties, she happily relented, lying back on the blanket and letting him discover her. When he kissed her breasts, she murmured her pleasure. When he kissed his way down her body, she groaned as need spiraled inside her. And when he finished his exploration by using his mouth on her intimately to grant her release, she cried out his name, lost in erotic bliss. . . .

When she finally floated back to earth, she found him grinning at her with a satisfied male expression. She couldn't help herself, she returned his smile.

"I knew we'd have fun," she said as soon as she could speak again.

"We've always had fun together." As Caitlin watched, he reached over and snagged his jeans off the floor, tugged out his wallet, and retrieved a couple of condoms.

Caitlin raised one eyebrow. "Have you been bringing other ladies up here and making them scream, Brent?"

He laughed and shook his head. "No. I bought the condoms after things started getting out of control with us. Seemed like the smart thing to do."

He silenced any other questions she might have by finding her lips and giving her a sizzling kiss. Again and again his tongue slipped inside her mouth. Caitlin was so focused on the kiss that it took a moment to realize she was beneath him, her body more than ready to accept him.

As her heart had. She could no longer fool herself by thinking this was about lust. What she felt with Brent went so much deeper than simply satisfying her body. This man filled her heart and her soul.

Caitlin cupped his head in her hands as he kissed her deeply. She buried her hands in his thick hair and closed her eyes. The sensations he created within her were magic. Magic that she knew wouldn't fade in her memory once she moved to Dallas. This time with Brent would stay with her for life.

He must have been feeling some of the same things,

because his expression was intense when he lifted his head and looked at her. Holding her gaze, he entered her slowly, joining their bodies.

"You feel wonderful," he said. Braced above her, he watched her as he thrust time and again into her. Caitlin felt the pressure build within her again, and she met each thrust as her need built. Looking up into Brent's face, loving the man who was bringing her so much pleasure, she touched the side of his face, emotions overcoming her. Brent leaned into her palm, his eyes fiery with passion.

"Caitlin," he said in a soft, reverent whisper.

The tenderness in his voice hurried Caitlin to her own climax. As she cried out and tensed beneath him, Brent thrust deep one last time, gathering her close as he found his own release.

Brent drifted back to earth slowly, knowing more had happened in this cabin today than just good, old-fashioned lust. He and Caitlin had truly made love.

And soon, all too soon, she was going to walk out of his life.

That thought cooled his blood. Moving off her, he quickly cleaned up, then joined her again on the blanket. Gathering her close so her back was to his front, he said, "You okay?"

Caitlin reached over and draped part of one of the blankets across her exposed body, shielding herself from his view.

Resisting the impulse to smile, he said, "You know, honey, I've seen you already. In fact, I've more than just seen your body. I've felt it. I've tasted it."

"Yes, I know. But I want to talk to you, and I can't do that if your mind is on something else."

He didn't bother to tell her that she could wrap

herself in a whole box of blankets and it wouldn't make a bit of difference. There was only one thing on his mind at the moment, and it wasn't talking.

But the lady was determined. She shifted, tugging on the blanket and endeavoring to stay wrapped, until she faced him.

"How did you get shot?" she asked.

Brent should have known she wouldn't forget. He might as well tell her the story. Caitlin wasn't the type to let go of things.

"A robbery in progress at a convenience store. The kid was high on drugs and heavily armed. Things got out of control, and I got shot. But we brought him in."

Caitlin leaned forward and placed her fingers against the scar. "Does it still hurt?"

"No." Brent captured her hand and moved it lower, wanting her to touch him where he truly ached. He sucked in a tight breath when she wrapped her fingers around his length. "Something good came out of it, though. I realized I wanted to come home and build a life here in Desmond."

He didn't admit to her that he now knew who he wanted that future with. Instead, before Caitlin could ask any more questions, he made love to her again, slower this time. He tried to show her with his touch and his kisses what she meant to him. And hoping, despite himself, that somehow, some way, he might find a way to change Caitlin's mind about leaving him. Because if he didn't, he knew the wound on his heart would never heal.

* * *

"I think with only a little more research, I can show how I'm related to England's royal family," Mabel Dawson announced the next afternoon as Caitlin and Brent stopped by with a hot meal.

Caitlin was glad to have someone else around to alleviate the tension in the air whenever she was with Brent. Things were awkward between them, and it was her fault. She knew they needed to talk about what had happened, but she wasn't prepared to do that. Not right now. Not when she was so confused.

They'd hardly spoken since their interlude at the cabin. After they'd made love a second time yesterday, Brent had driven her home. He'd walked her to her doorstep, but before they could discuss what they'd shared, she gave him a quick kiss and slipped inside her apartment.

She was a coward, and she knew it.

But what would be the point in talking about this? One conversation wouldn't make things better, and it sure as heck wouldn't help her with her main problem. She was in love with Brent. After yesterday, she could no longer pretend she was anything but completely, madly, foolishly in love with him.

Which was the worst possible thing that could happen to her.

Focusing back on Mabel, Caitlin suppressed her own unsettling thoughts. "English royalty, huh? That's pretty good."

"It will be, but I don't have time to look into it right now. I'm knitting for the Hirsch children."

Caitlin studied the needlework in the older woman's hands. Mabel was making a tiny pink sweater. It would look great on little Katie when the weather turned cold in a couple of months.

"This sweater is wonderful." Caitlin sat next to Mabel on the couch, her gaze on the knitting. Noticing a larger dark blue sweater, she picked it up. It was obviously for Peter, and looked like something a member of the Dallas Cowboys football team would wear.

"Do you think the children will like these?" Mabel asked.

"They'll love them." Caitlin glanced quickly at Brent and then away. She remembered all too well how it felt to be in his arms, to have him kiss her, caress her, make her feel cherished and special and—

Arrgh! No. She wasn't going to do this. She wasn't going to turn to mush and lose sight of her dreams. She had to keep her priorities straight. What mattered was her new job and the opportunities it would offer her. She'd wanted this chance for such a long time. She couldn't just throw it away. No, she needed to concentrate on the job and not think about anything else.

"The sweaters are terrific." Brent lifted the one for Peter. "What gave you the idea to make them?"

Mabel patted Caitlin's hand. "Caitlin did."

That got her attention. "I did not."

With a laugh, Mabel said, "Sure you did. Last year, when I was having so many health problems, you got the Girl Scouts to make me bouquets of tissue paper roses. Those flowers and the thoughtful girls who made them brightened my days. So naturally, when Caitlin mentioned the Hirsch family, I knew their days would be brighter if I made them a little something, too."

Brent settled into the chair facing the couch. Since his gaze was intent on Mabel, Caitlin gave in to temptation and used this opportunity to study him. He was so good-looking, no wonder she'd fallen in love with him. But there was much more to him than his looks.

"It's nice of you to do this," Brent said.

Mabel smiled. "Maybe. But I've had a lot of fun doing it. That's the beauty of Good Neighbors. Someone does something for me, like bring me hot meals now and again. Then I do something else for someone else, like knit a sweater or two. It all works out in the end." She turned to look at Caitlin. "Except when it comes to you. I don't think anyone does anything for you."

Mabel's comment really surprised Caitlin. "I don't need anything," she said.

"Sure you do. This town just hasn't figured out what it is yet." Mabel picked up the pink sweater. "Would you two mind stopping by in a couple of days and taking these sweaters to the Hirsches?"

"Sure. But why don't we bring the Hirsch family here instead?" Brent asked. "That way, you can meet the kids yourself."

Ah, now why did he have to be such a nice guy? Mabel loved nothing more than company, and having the Hirsches stop by would really make her day. Not surprisingly, the old lady quickly agreed to Brent's plan, and the remainder of their visit was spent calling Alice Hirsh and figuring out when she and her children would be free to visit.

As Brent made the arrangements, Caitlin realized he didn't really need her around anymore. Sure, there were still a couple of fine points about Good Neighbors he might not know, but for the most part, the man could take over today.

Which meant, over the next few days before her move, she could spend more time getting ready to leave . . . and less time with Brent. Deep in her heart, she knew spending less time with him was an excellent idea. She also knew it wasn't going to help with her main problem—loving Brent.

Darn it all. Why couldn't she just simply lust after him? Now what was she supposed to do?

As they left Mabel's apartment a while later, Caitlin said, "That was a sweet idea you had about inviting the Hirsches over."

They had reached his Suburban, and as Brent unlocked it, he glanced at her. "Actually, it wasn't sweet. It was calculated. Mabel has a nice little income between her teacher's pension and Social Security, but she could use some help around the house. Alice Hirsch needs money and could probably do a great job cleaning Mabel's house once a week and cooking up some meals. And while Alice is doing that, Mabel can visit with the children."

"That's a great idea," Caitlin said after they were seated inside his car. "I'm impressed."

The look Brent gave her was nothing short of incendiary. It heated her blood and reminded her all too well what had happened between them yesterday.

"Don't be impressed." Reaching over, he lightly stroked her cheek. "I'm just trying to do what you would do." When his gaze dropped to her lips, she knew he was thinking about kissing her. Which, as much as she hated admitting it, she wanted him to do.

"I do have one question, though," he said softly, leaning toward her ever so slightly. "What is it that you need?"

Caitlin blinked. "What?"

"Mabel said the town hasn't figured out yet what you needed. So, tell me, what do you need?"

I need you.

That answer jumped right into Caitlin's mind, but she squelched it. No, no, no. She didn't need Brent. She needed her freedom. And her brand-new job in Dallas. She didn't need Brent, who at this very moment was moving closer, obviously with the intention of kissing her.

Which was a really, really, bad idea. She summoned up what little self-control she had and leaned away from him.

"Yesterday was a mistake," she said bluntly. "A big mistake."

Rather than being offended by her comment, Brent calmly started the car. "Really? You think so? I kinda thought it was pretty fantastic."

"Sure, it was fantastic, but I'm leaving."

Calmly, he turned down the street where their houses were. "You've made that clear. I haven't asked you to change your mind. It wouldn't be right for me to ask you."

He seemed so calm, so in control that she couldn't help thinking that something was up with him.

"Brent Stewart, you expect me to believe that we made love yesterday and you're okay with me packing up and leaving in a few days? I know you better than that."

Brent parked his car in his driveway, then turned to face her. "You're looking forward to living in Dallas, aren't you?"

The non sequitur caught her off guard. "Yes. But I'm really looking forward to starting my new job, helping all those people. What does that have to do with yesterday?''

Rather than answering her question, he asked, ''What would you do if I moved to Dallas to be near you?''

He could have slapped her in the face with a fish and not surprised her more. ''Excuse me? You can't be serious.''

''What if I were? What would you do?''

''You hated Dallas.''

His gaze was intense. ''But I like you.''

''Like?''

He lifted one eyebrow. ''Do you want me to be more honest than that?''

''No,'' she blurted, shoving open her door. ''No, I don't want either of us to be more honest than that.''

Then before he could say anything else, she headed toward her apartment, wanting to get away from Brent and the temptation he offered quickly before she did something really stupid—like tell him she loved him.

Brent smiled as he watched Caitlin walk away. She was in love with him. He knew it. He'd known it yesterday when they'd made love. Despite everything she'd said, yesterday hadn't been about lust. It had been love. Pure and simple. Wonderful and wild.

They'd made love because they were in love. He knew it. She knew it. She just wasn't happy about it.

Now his problem was how to change her mind and convince her that being in love was a wonderful thing, not an awful mess. Was there any way to prove that their love could make her happy, not ruin her life? And how did he show her that life in Desmond could be exciting?

Brent knew he needed help. Mabel's words came back to him. She'd said the town hadn't done anything for Caitlin yet because folks hadn't figured out what she needed. If he asked, would they show Caitlin how they felt about her? Everyone talked about how much they wished she wasn't leaving, but what if they had to put their money where their mouths were? What if he asked them to help him show Caitlin how much she meant to them?

Warming to his idea, Brent couldn't help wondering what would happen if he could make Caitlin's dreams come true right here in Desmond. If he tried, and had the help of everyone in town, maybe he could change Caitlin's mind. And if they showed her how much she meant to them, what would happen then? Would she stay?

Or would she still go?

Well, there was only one way to find out, and Brent wasn't going to waste any more time.

Caitlin bit back a yawn and stared at the troop of Girl Scouts standing on the narrow landing in front of her apartment. It was eight o'clock on a Saturday morning. What in the world were they doing here?

"Morning, girls," she said with another yawn. "Was I supposed to help your troop with something today?"

"No. We just wanted to give you this," the smallest one said, shoving a huge bouquet of wildflowers into Caitlin's hands. "This is because we 'preciate everything you do for us."

Caitlin stared at the flowers, taken aback. What in the world had prompted this? She hadn't done anything special. Sure, she'd helped them find a meeting place, but that hadn't been a big deal. And, okay, she might have helped out a little with their cookie drive last year. But that had been all. Well, pretty much all.

"Girls, this is so sweet of you," Caitlin said, fighting the tightness in her throat. She looked at the flowers again. It had been a long time since anyone had given her flowers, and the fact that these girls had all gotten up early to pick wildflowers for her warmed her heart.

"We just wanted you to know," a second girl piped up, "we think you're great."

"Plus, we're going to miss you when you're gone," a tall brunette added from the back of the group.

With that pronouncement, the girls turned and noisily clumped down the stairs leading to Caitlin's apartment. Caitlin stepped out of her doorway and watched them descend. A couple of moms stood at the bottom of the stairs. They waved brightly to Caitlin, then hustled the girls back into two waiting minivans.

Caitlin glanced over at Brent's house. There was no sign of him, which wasn't surprising. Eight o'clock in the morning was the middle of the day to an early riser like Brent. Still, Caitlin wished he were home so she could show him what the girls had done for her. What a special way to start the day.

But as the day wore on, the flowers weren't the only special thing to happen. Midmorning, when she went to pick up her Sunday dress at the dry cleaners, the owner, Mickey Turner, waved away her money, saying it was on the house this time. But the biggest surprise came when she got to the Good Neighbors office in the basement of city hall. Her old metal desk was covered with packages of all shapes and sizes.

Dumbfounded, Caitlin wandered over and inspected the stack.

"This entire town has lost its collective mind," she said, sitting and reading a few of the notes attached to the presents. They all said pretty much the same thing—*thanks. Thanks for helping. Thanks for caring. Thanks for being there.*

And they all said one more thing—*we'll miss you when you're gone.*

"Whoa, what did you do? Mug Santa?" her brother, Al, asked from the doorway.

Caitlin turned and looked at him. "Can you believe this? These are all thank-you presents."

Al walked inside her office and sat in the lone chair facing her desk. "Well, you deserve every one. It's about time someone did something for you."

Okay, she hadn't fallen off the pumpkin truck yesterday. She could smell a conspiracy a mile off. "Do you know something about this?"

Al shook his head. "Nope. Not me. But then I'm usually the last to know about anything."

That was true, at least. Al had been practically the last one in town to find out his wife was pregnant. Of course, since Madeline had bought a home pregnancy kit at Miller's Drug Store, what did he expect? Still, Caitlin couldn't shake the feeling that her brother knew more about this than he was letting on.

"Tell me the truth, Al. What's this about?"

Al looked her straight in the eye. "No one has told me anything about this," he said. And Caitlin believed him. Al wasn't a good liar; everyone knew that, so if there were some sort of method to this madness, no one would tell him about it.

"So if you're not in on this, what are you doing here?"

"Thought you might want to go to the Demons game tonight. Madeline doesn't feel up to it, but the game's supposed to be a killer."

Aw, her brother's favorite sport—football. He'd played on the local high school team, the Demons, himself and now he never missed a game unless he had to.

Caitlin shifted her gaze back to the pile of presents on her desk. She might as well go to the game. Most of the town would be there, and she could use the opportunity to thank everyone for their gifts. Maybe she could also learn why they had done this.

"Sure, I'll come to the game," she said absently.

Al chuckled. "Let it go, Caitlin. There's no big town-wide conspiracy dedicated to giving you presents."

As much as Caitlin wanted to believe him, she wasn't so sure. Especially when she got to the football game and found that special seats had been saved for her, her brother, and Brent on the fifty-yard line.

"What's going on?" Caitlin demanded of Brent as soon as he sat next to her.

"Going on where?"

Exasperated, Caitlin waved at their seats. "Here. And at my apartment. And at the Good Neighbors office. Everyone is acting loopy today. People are giving me presents, picking wildflowers for me. It's . . . weird."

Brent gave her a slow, easy smile that made her heart race. "Maybe they're trying to show you what you mean to them. I wouldn't worry about it. You must know this entire town is in love with you."

His words made her breath catch in her throat. Was the entire town in love with her? Really? Did that include him?

No, wait. She didn't want him to answer that question. No sir, not at all. Not one little bit. Because if he loved her, and she loved him, well, that would be too much for her to deal with. It was much better to think that Brent still happily believed that what they'd shared was simple lust. That way, when she moved away, she wouldn't have to wonder if she'd hurt him.

But glancing at him now, she met and held his gaze. It was sweet and tender and made her feel happy and sad at the same time.

Ah, darn it all. He was in love with her. She could see it in his beautiful eyes. Almost as if he sensed her mood, he reached over and took her hand in his.

For the first half of the game, she held on to him. Just this once, she didn't want to think about tomorrow and her future and what Dallas would be like. She only wanted to sit here, in the cool fall night, watching the football game and holding the hand of the man she loved, whether she should or not.

But as the first half ended, all thoughts of loving Brent disappeared from her mind. Instead, she watched befuddled as the entire football team lined up, and with the musical accompaniment of the Desmond marching band, put on a half-time show by singing "You Light Up My Life." Off-key. To Caitlin.

Oh, no.

Chapter Eight

Brent stood in his kitchen doorway and watched Caitlin park in her driveway. He knew it was only a matter of time before she came over to talk to him, so he figured he might as well just wait. The lady was full of questions.

And she wanted answers from him.

After the football team's serenade, she'd asked him again and again if he knew what was going on. He'd denied knowing, mostly because he didn't want to go into it in front of all of Desmond. But Caitlin hadn't swallowed his line. He'd clearly seen in her pretty eyes that she knew he was in on this, and she wasn't about to let it drop.

Sure enough, as soon as she got out of her compact car, she headed across the grass toward his house.

"If Dad wasn't out of town, I'd ask him to interrogate you," she said when she stood in front of him.

Brent moved back so she could enter the house. Once inside, she sat at the kitchen table and leveled her gaze on him.

"I can't stand it," she said. "Tell me the truth. Either I've gone crazy or the rest of this town has. What in blue blazes is going on?"

Her words brought a smile to his face. "The people in Desmond want you to know how much you mean to them. It's that simple."

Caitlin's look was dubious. "Simple? Doesn't seem simple to me. Seems like an organized plan to get me to change my mind about leaving."

She was smart. Very smart. "What if it were?"

Her sigh was deep and heartfelt. "It won't make any difference, Brent. Whatever they do, I'm still going. It's sweet, but I need this job. I want this job. I thought you understood."

He felt lost and lonely all over again. Yeah, he understood why the new job was important to her.

Reaching across the table, he covered her hand with his. "These gestures will just make all of us in town feel better. We'll get a chance before you go to say thank you for what you've done."

She turned her hand and wove her fingers between his. "Ah, Brent, leaving Desmond was so simple before you came back to town."

Her touch, as always, heated his blood. Images of the two of them together made his heart pound. He wanted her again, and when she lifted her gaze to his, he watched with fascination as her eyes darkened with passion.

"We've never really talked about it," Brent said.

"About what?" Her voice was soft, husky.

"Caitlin, we made love. We can't ignore what's happening between us."

Her smile was rueful. "We can if we try."

"Maybe I don't want to."

She removed her hand from his and stood, pacing the room. "What do you expect me to do, Brent? Stay here in Desmond? Marry you? Raise a family? Even though I . . . care deeply for you, I can't. That's your dream, not mine."

"I know," he admitted. "I know you want to leave. Everyone in town knows you want to leave. This is just our way of saying good-bye."

She stopped pacing when she stood directly in front of him. "So this is your idea?"

"No. Actually, if you remember, Mabel brought it up. I just happened to mention to some people that maybe we should do a few things to show you how we all felt before you left."

"Brent!" She started pacing again. "So what other things do I have to look forward to?"

He chuckled. "Now if I told you that, the town would never forgive me."

She looked at him, narrowing her eyes. "It's not going to work, you know. I'm not going to change my mind about this move. In two days, I'm going to Dallas for some meetings and to finalize the details. This is my dream, Brent. I've thought about it for a long time. I don't want to end up with a lot of regrets."

Knowing she was leaving so soon really bothered him, but since he loved her, he wanted her to have what she wanted. Still, as sneaky as it seemed, he couldn't help wishing all those thoughtful gestures would somehow show her it was possible to have those dreams right here in Desmond.

"Everyone knows you're not changing your mind, but let us do a few things for you before you leave," he said.

He watched emotions chase across her face. Finally, with a sigh, she said, "It won't hurt anything, I guess. And it is very nice." She walked over to the door. "Just so I can prepare, you have to tell me how many more gestures are coming my way."

Standing, Brent crossed the room, stopping a few inches away from her. He could smell her perfume, and as always, need coiled through him. "I'll just say a lot of people want to do something for you."

He alone had two or three things planned, so did her brothers. Then there were other people who'd been helped by Good Neighbors who wanted to say thanks. As far as he could tell, Caitlin was in for quite a few gestures between now and when she left for those meetings in Dallas. But that probably wasn't the answer she wanted to hear at this moment.

Groaning, Caitlin looked up at him. "Brent, you know if I could live my life in Desmond without regrets, I would. But I can't."

"I know." Unable to resist touching her any longer, he reached out and ran his fingertips across her jaw. "Just as you know if I could live my life in Dallas without regrets, I would. But I can't."

Caitlin's gaze was intense. "I know," she said, her voice a mere whisper in the room.

Brent wasn't sure which of them moved first, but the next thing he knew, she was in his arms. Their kiss was about passion and longing and dreams and regrets. It was deep and urgent, and Brent couldn't remember a kiss touching his soul like this one did. Soon, desire overwhelmed all other emotions, and he slipped his hands under her T-shirt, finding and caressing her soft, full breasts.

"We shouldn't do this," Caitlin murmured against his lips, her own hands wandering across his body. "We just agreed I'm leaving."

Brent trailed a string of ardent kisses down the side of her neck. "If you're expecting me to be the strong one here, forget it. I've got no willpower where you're concerned."

"Me neither." Caitlin sought his lips, and slipped her tongue inside his mouth.

Her kiss seared him down to his toes. He returned it, pulling her closer so she could feel how much he wanted her. He cupped her breasts again and stroked her taut nipples through the silky material of her bra. Desire surged through him, and he felt his common sense slipping away. When she rubbed against him, he moaned, knowing things were about to get crazy.

"One of us had better stop this, because I'm about two seconds away from carrying you to my bedroom," he murmured.

Caitlin leaned back and looked at him. "You truly understand that I'm leaving, right?"

He wasn't sure where she was going with this but he answered anyway. "Yeah. I understand."

"Good. Then we're in agreement—what we're about to do is a huge mistake, and it doesn't mean anything." Looking around, she asked, "So which way is your bedroom?"

Caitlin sat in the Good Neighbors office the next afternoon wondering if she could get herself committed. After all, she had to be crazy, right? Why else would she have made love with Brent . . . again. But she had. And for all intents and purposes, it had been her idea. All she'd needed to do was tell Brent no. Heck, maybe if she'd stopped kissing him like there was no tomorrow, that would have given him the idea, too.

But no. She'd kissed him as if there were no waiting job in Dallas. As if there were nothing keeping them apart. What had she been thinking? Making love with Brent only made her fall harder for him. Wasn't it enough that she was going to miss him unbelievably when she got to Dallas? Did she need to make herself miserable, too?

The problem was, she couldn't resist him. Leaning back in her desk chair, she debated her situation. Maybe this was one of those cases where it was all in how you looked at it. Brent knew she was leaving. Heck, they both knew that. So if they knew that, then why couldn't they just accept the fact and enjoy the time they had together? Maybe, instead of being miserable, she'd be happy she had so many wonderful memories of Brent when she got to Dallas.

Plus, there was another upside to making love with him. Since she didn't want to miss any opportunities in life, enjoying their romance while she could was better than ending up regretting not being with him. Or was she just rationalizing this because she couldn't seem to keep her mittens off the man?

"You are an idiot in need of a village," she muttered to herself.

Not that she was about to change her mind, of course. Because last night had rocked her world. Making love with Brent was wild and tender and wonderful and amazing . . . and she wasn't about to walk away from it a moment before she had to. Okay, it probably wasn't a smart move, but she wasn't feeling particularly smart at the moment.

Well, what was the worst thing that could happen? Oh, right. She'd end up missing Brent. But it was inevitable she'd miss him, so she might as well enjoy the time they had. Then, when she got to Dallas and was busy with her new job, she could at least look back on this brief affair as one opportunity she hadn't let pass her by.

Picking up the phone, she dialed Brent's house. She wanted to explain her thinking on this and see if he agreed. Caitlin smiled at the thought. Yeah, right. Like he was going to say no. Brent had been the one keeping her in his bed this morning. Long after she would have gone home, he'd used his considerable skill to persuade her to stay. No way would Brent turn her down.

"I don't think it's a good idea," Brent said twenty minutes later as he leaned against the doorjamb to her office. He couldn't believe Caitlin was suggesting this, although he shouldn't be surprised after last night. He hadn't meant for it to happen. He'd vowed not to make love with her again.

But he hadn't been able to stop himself. And today, well up until two seconds ago when she'd outlined her plan, he'd hoped that maybe their incredible night together might have changed her mind about leaving.

Instead, she was telling him how in some ways, their being together made it easier for her to leave.

"You're kidding, right? Why do you think it's a bad idea? What harm can it do to continue . . ."

"Making love?" He took a step inside her office and shut the door behind him. "Don't you think it might make it even more difficult for us to say good-bye when it's time for you to leave? Last night meant a lot to me, Caitlin. Didn't it mean anything to you?"

"We both agreed beforehand that it didn't mean anything. Not really."

How could she say that? "I don't care what we agreed. It meant a lot."

Caitlin shrugged, but he could read her answer in her eyes. Last night had meant a lot to her, too. "Maybe. But what do you suggest we do? Spend the next few days wanting to make love but not doing it? How does that help anything? My way, at least we get to enjoy the time we have together."

"I don't know. This just seems wrong," he said.

Wearing a smile he knew spelled trouble for him, she circled her desk and came to stand next to him. "Oh, come on, Brent. Be a buddy. Have hot, fantastic, passionate sex with me for the next few days. Pretty please?"

He couldn't help it. He laughed. And gave up any hope of resisting her. Turning, he slipped his arms loosely around her waist and gave her a kiss. Why couldn't this be what she wanted? To stay here with him? Why couldn't their love be enough?

But it wasn't. And he knew that.

Before either of them could deepen the kiss, he lifted his head.

"Oh, okay. But just so you know, you're the only woman I'd do this for."

She grinned up at him. "I should hope so."

When she leaned up to kiss him again, he stopped her. "I have something fun planned for us this afternoon, and I don't want to get distracted by kissing and fooling around in your office."

"What could possibly be more fun than fooling around in my office?"

"First, I'm taking you on a hot-air balloon ride."

She blinked at him. "You're what?"

"I thought I'd put a little excitement in your life. You remember Jake Swanson? You helped his son find a job? Jake told me last week he has a hot-air balloon, and he offered to take us for a ride. Want to go?"

"Yes. Of course. But is Jake sure he wants to do this? I mean, I didn't really do much for him. I just—"

"Found his son a job when no one would hire him. You did a lot for that young man and his family, Caitlin, and Jake would like to do something in return for you. Accept it."

Caitlin nodded. "Fine. It's very sweet of Jake, and it sounds like fun." After a brief hesitation, she added, "You said first. That *first* we were going on the hot-air balloon ride. That means there's more than just the ride. What else is going to happen?"

Brent gave her a grin, feeling optimistic about the day he had planned for them. "Oh, there are a few other surprises. But we'll talk about them as the day goes on," he said.

One way or another, he was going to prove a couple of things to Caitlin—one, that a lot of people loved her, and two, that you didn't have to go to Dallas to find excitement. Desmond, Texas offered a lot of excitement, too.

* * *

Caitlin leaned back in the plush seat of the limousine and took another sip of her champagne. No doubt about it, Brent knew how to put together an exciting day. The hot-air balloon ride had been thrilling and amazing and a tiny bit scary. She'd had a terrific time and had thought that would be the high point of her day.

But she'd underestimated Brent. After bringing her home from the hot-air balloon ride, he'd announced he'd arranged to take her to dinner and a play in Tyler. If that wasn't enough, he'd also arranged for them to be driven the forty miles in a limousine. It seemed Reverend Williams had a cousin who owned a limousine company and was happy to make the evening special for Caitlin and Brent.

Now how in the world was she supposed to resist not only Brent but also an entire town? She might have a chance of resisting the town, but hoo-boy, not Brent in a tux. Yummy, yummy, yummy. That she couldn't resist.

"Did you enjoy the balloon ride?" Brent asked.

"It was wonderful."

"And the dinner?"

"Equally wonderful. As was the play." She finished the champagne in her glass, then smiled warmly at him. "This champagne is pretty wonderful, too."

Brent reached over and took the glass from her hand. "You don't drink much, do you?"

She smiled. "Now why do you say that?"

"Because you look all fluffy and warm after only one glass."

"The drink had nothing to do with how I'm feeling." She smiled at him again, and this time he returned her smile. As always, it made her heart beat faster. "I'm all dressed up in my fanciest clothes riding around in a limousine with a gorgeous man. Why wouldn't I feel fluffy and warm?"

His chuckle was deep and warmed her all over. "Caitlin Rogers, are you flirting with me?"

"You betcha. Or at least I'm trying. Is it working?"

The look he gave her left her in no doubt that he was feeling the chemistry between them every bit as much as she was. "Yeah. It's working." He undid his bow tie and let it hang loose around his neck. "And that dress isn't hurting either."

Thrilled that he liked her simple black dress, Caitlin decided she was in the mood for a little fun and games. He sat a couple of feet from her on the wide backseat. He was too far away, in Caitlin's opinion. And since her opinion seemed to be the only one that mattered tonight, she might as well do something about this.

She kicked off her shoes. Then, turning as much as her seat belt would let her, she plopped her stocking-clad legs in his lap. Brent raised one eyebrow and settled his hands around her calves. "Want me to rub your feet?"

"That's as good a place as any to start."

Brent's gaze never wavered from her own as he tenderly massaged first her feet, then up her legs. Slowly, expertly, he lulled her into a sensuous state of need and longing. By the time his hands skimmed over her knees and slipped beneath the hem of her dress, Caitlin felt like screaming with pent-up desire.

Instead, she remained perfectly still as he inched his hands higher, caressing her flesh beneath her silky

hose. Apparently, he'd expected her to be wearing
pantyhose, because when he reached the tops of her
stockings and touched bare skin, he stopped.

"You're wearing stockings. And a garter belt." His
voice was husky, rough, as his fingertips trailed across
her exposed thighs.

"Um. I thought you might like them." With his
warm touch on her bare skin, Caitlin had to admit,
she was enjoying the stockings, too. She especially
liked the sizzling look in his eyes.

"Caitlin, I love them," he said as he slid his hands
up higher until they rested on the delicate panties
at the juncture of her thighs.

Caitlin sucked in a tight breath as his fingers ex-
plored her. "Brent, I don't think—"

It took a moment for the intruding noise to sink
through the sensual haze that had settled over her.
Then she realized her cell phone was ringing in her
purse.

"No," Brent said, pulling his hands out from under
her dress. He leaned down to snag her purse before
she could, but he was too late. "Tonight is about you,
Caitlin. Other Good Neighbors volunteers can cover
whatever the problem is."

As much as she was tempted to do as he suggested
and let the call go, Caitlin knew whoever was calling
wouldn't be doing so if they really didn't need her
help.

"I promise it won't ruin our evening," she assured
Brent as she slipped her phone out of her purse. "I'll
only be a minute."

Brent sighed and leaned against the back of the
seat. Caitlin blew him a kiss, then answered her
phone.

"Hello," Caitlin said, keeping her gaze on Brent. He looked like a man fighting sexual frustration. She knew exactly how he felt.

"Caitlin," the little voice on the other end of the phone line said. "Katie's really sick."

Caitlin's heart jumped into her throat. "Peter, honey, is your mommy there?"

"She's trying to cool Katie down in the tub." Peter hiccupped around a sob. "Mommy said I shouldn't call you, but I'm scared."

Caitlin was scared, too. She looked at Brent, who must have sensed the urgency of the call. She covered the receiver and quickly told him what Peter had said. Then she said to the little boy, "Can your mommy come to the phone?"

She heard voices in the background. After a few seconds, Peter returned to the line. "Mommy says everything is okay, and that I shouldn't have called you. Sorry, Caitlin."

"Peter, wait—" But it was too late. The little boy had hung up. Turning to Brent, she started to explain how she felt it was important they swing by the Hirsches, just to make certain baby Katie really was okay.

But she didn't have to say a word. Brent was in the process of giving the driver directions to the Hirsches' house. She knew Brent had to be disappointed the evening was ending this way. He'd gone to a lot of trouble to make tonight magical. Yet without a word, he'd ditched their plans to check on a little boy and his sick baby sister.

"Thank you," Caitlin said, touched by his thoughtfulness.

Brent shook his head. "I'm doing this for Peter. You don't have to thank me."

Leaning over, she kissed him soundly. "Yes. I do. It means a lot to me that you're a nice guy."

The look he gave her was pure bad boy. "Oh, I'm not that nice. I intend to take up where we left off as soon as we leave the Hirsches."

She certainly hoped he meant that.

Alice Hirsh sighed as she opened the door, with Katie crying in her arms. "I told Peter not to call you. Especially not tonight. I heard you two have special plans."

"We don't mind." Brent placed his hand on Katie's forehead. She felt hot, but not as feverish as he'd expected. "What's wrong with the baby?"

"Ear infection. We saw the pediatrician this afternoon, and he started her on antibiotics. But I still need to keep her fever down." Alice rocked the baby in her arms, her gaze studying their clothes. "Everything's fine. Really. I just want to make certain she doesn't get too hot. You two don't have to stay."

Brent glanced at Caitlin, who smiled at him. As much as he wanted to get her alone, he couldn't just walk away from the Hirsch family. Especially once Peter appeared next to his mother.

"Sorry I called you," he muttered, looking down at his sneakers.

"That's okay. We don't mind," Brent assured him.

"Why don't we just stick around for a little while? I'm sure you could use some help," Caitlin said.

Alice looked unsure. "I don't want to ruin your evening."

"You're not ruining it," Brent assured her.

When Alice relented, Brent and Caitlin both headed inside the small house. Brent shrugged out of his jacket as they went. There was no way they were leaving until they knew the baby was fine.

Which, eventually, she was. For the next couple of hours, he and Caitlin pitched in, helping Alice. When she called the pediatrician just to make certain Katie was okay, he told them they didn't need to go to the hospital unless Katie's temperature climbed higher than 102°.

Peter hovered over his little sister. His dedication touched Brent's heart, and as always when he was around Peter, the desire for children filled him. He glanced at Caitlin. What he wouldn't give to have those children with her. But that wasn't going to happen, so he might as well accept reality.

It was very late when they left the Hirsch family. The limousine driver had fallen asleep in the front seat. After waking him, they headed home, bone-tired but happy the baby was asleep and on the mend.

After the limousine dropped them off in front of his house, Brent silently walked Caitlin over to her apartment. The night was clear, and he drew a deep breath of Texas air into his lungs. Before he could say anything to Caitlin, she reached down and took his hand in hers.

"Come upstairs to my apartment," she said softly.

He didn't argue because, hell, he'd follow her to the ends of the earth if that was where she wanted to go.

"We definitely should talk." He ignored the seductive smile she gave him. No, they were going to talk. At least a little bit. Tomorrow, she was headed to

Dallas for those meetings. He was running out of time to tell her what he felt.

When they got upstairs to her apartment, she turned on one of the table lamps and sat on the sofa. Brent sat near her, while still leaving enough space between them for his peace of mind. He needed that space if he wanted to stay focused on the conversation.

"I'll start," she said. "I've already told you that today was wonderful. The last couple of days have been crazy and fun, and I really appreciate everything you and the people in town did for me."

He had to level with her. It was now or never. "We're all hoping to show you that life in Desmond can be exciting, too."

"Why?"

"Maybe you'll change your mind about leaving."

She sighed, but didn't look surprised or angry. "But we've been through this. I'm not changing my mind."

Brent sucked in a tight breath and went for broke. "Even if I tell you I love you?"

"Oh, Brent. Don't."

"Don't what? Don't be in love with you? Because I can't help that, Caitlin."

When her gaze met his, he realized with a start that her eyes had filled with tears.

"Don't tell me. How can I leave knowing I'm breaking your heart?" she asked.

For the first time in a long time, hope filled him. "Then don't leave."

He was a jerk for even asking her, but he couldn't help himself. He couldn't let her move away without knowing how he felt. He also couldn't let her leave without knowing how she felt about him.

"Do you feel anything for me?" he asked.

She leaned back against the sofa and closed her eyes. When she finally opened them, sadness filled their depths.

"Can we talk about this when I get back from Dallas?" Her soft voice tore at his heart. As much as he didn't want to wait, he knew he had to. Pressuring Caitlin now was unfair.

"Sure. We can wait." He stood, intending to leave, but she stopped him.

He braced himself, expecting her to ask him to make love with her, but she didn't ask a thing. Instead, she gave him a slow, sultry kiss that melted his resolve. When she headed toward the bedroom, he followed, all the while calling himself the biggest fool on the planet. Making love settled nothing between them, but when it came to Caitlin, he was powerless to resist.

Powerless to resist the feeling of oneness that came over him when she kissed him. Powerless to resist the desire that heated his blood when they both helped each other out of their clothes. And powerless to resist the love he saw in her eyes when he gathered her close.

"I like the stockings," he murmured, nuzzling her neck and backing her toward the bed.

She still had them on, and the sight of her legs in the sheer hose that ended in lacy bands around her thighs was pushing him beyond endurance.

"You can take them off, it you want."

"Maybe later. With my teeth," he said as they tumbled onto the soft mattress. Okay, so making love wasn't going to solve anything, but he could show her how much she meant to him. With his touch. With his kisses. With his body.

They were hungry for each other, stoking a fire already raging out of control. It didn't take long before her caresses got to him, and he fumbled in his pants pocket for his wallet.

"I've got to put these things somewhere easier to get at," he muttered when it took him a while to retrieve a foil packet and sheathe himself with a condom.

Caitlin lay on the bed, looking at him. Love filled him, and with all the tenderness of his heart, he moved between her legs and drove into her.

Her small gasp of pleasure encouraged him. Again and again he thrust into her, feeling her body wrap around him the same way she'd wrapped around his heart.

When her cries became urgent, he increased the pace, finally pushing her over the edge. At the moment of her release, she cried out his name and a few words more. "I love you, too."

That was enough to send him soaring over the edge after her.

Chapter Nine

Caitlin's feet hurt. Badly. She shifted her weight, hoping to relieve some of the pain her too-new pumps were giving her, but to no avail. She'd spent too many hours walking from meeting to meeting for her shoes to forgive her. They were out for revenge, plain and simple, and she had no choice but to suffer in silence.

Some of her discomfort must have shown on her face, because Ann Moss, the woman who would soon be her manager at the Henderson Charity, gave her a sympathetic smile before she headed out of the meeting room and down the hall to her office. Caitlin followed, doing her best to keep up. But the pain from her shoes really was intense.

"Every day won't be as bad as this one," Ann said as they walked. "But since we're going to assign you to help with fund-raising, you will spend some of your time meeting people."

"But I'll also get to do some hands-on work, right? I'd really like to be in the field."

Ann smiled. "Well, we'll figure it out in the next few months. Don't worry. It's not a chore. I really enjoy our fund-raising trips."

They had reached Ann's office, and Caitlin gratefully sat in one of the chairs in front of the desk. Gingerly, she moved her toes, hoping to ease the pain. Instead, it got worse.

"I'm not sure I'm the fund-raising type," Caitlin admitted, surveying Ann's office. Although it wasn't big, it had a nice view out the window. Earlier in the day, Ann had shown her an empty office—with an equally nice view—that would be hers.

"Nonsense. You're a natural at fund-raising. Everyone loved you today."

They loved her. . . .

Not really. Not the way Brent did. Caitlin was still ashamed at the way she'd snuck out of her apartment this morning, leaving him asleep in her bed. But hey, what was she supposed to say to him? *Sure, I'll give up the job of a lifetime to stay in Desmond with you?* Forget about making a difference in the world? Forget excitement? Forget travel?

She didn't want to think about any of that right now. She had two more meetings this afternoon. And after that, some of the employees were taking her to dinner at her hotel. If it weren't for her too-tight shoes, she'd be having a great time. A terrific time.

The Henderson Charity was the right place for her. She was going to have the opportunity to help countless people.

So why wasn't she happy? She decided not to think about it now.

"What if I discover I'm not cut out for fund-raising? Do I have to continue doing it?" Caitlin asked Ann.

Ann laughed. "Not if you don't want to, but a lot of people like the challenge. And don't forget the travel. You get to go all over the country while still doing good. It's the best of both worlds. Most days, you'll get to do some field work. But our corporate liaison division raises most of our operating budget, and we need every penny. Money solves lots of problems in this world."

Caitlin knew Ann was right. Money did solve a lot of problems, and she'd certainly never had any at her disposal with Good Neighbors. Of course, she really hadn't needed any. She'd been able to get most everything necessary simply by asking. Bartering had worked well, too.

But a charity the size of Henderson could hardly barter for what was needed. They needed income, and lots of it, to keep their programs running. Those trips would give her a chance to spread the word about the good things the charity did.

"This afternoon, I'm going to introduce you to some of the folks on your team. To get you up to speed, Kenny will give you an overview of our department. And after that, Donna will fill you in on our corporate donors around the country. After you start next week, you, Donna, and Kenny will be visiting one of those companies. OptiTech just raised over a million dollars for Henderson during their last employee contribution campaign. You three will attend the banquet they're holding in San Francisco to mark the occasion."

Wow. San Francisco. Caitlin had always wanted to go there, and had never really expected to. But in a little over a week, she'd be there. Talk about exciting. Suddenly the pain in her feet didn't bother her as much.

Of course, she still didn't seem to be able to shake her heartache. Caitlin sighed inwardly. She just needed to accept that although she loved Brent, they weren't meant to be together.

Simple, really. With time, she'd get over him. Just like Brent would get over her, too. Heck, probably faster than a bunny could procreate. Mary Beth certainly had made it more than clear she was interested in him. And no doubt there were lots of other women around Desmond who would be happy to put his broken heart back together. They'd come to his house with casseroles and sympathetic smiles.

Those little—

Yikes. Where'd that come from? Caitlin shoved away the upsetting jealousy and concentrated on the conversation at hand. She would be happy about this job. She would. "I'm dying to see San Francisco."

"Oh, you're going to see lots of places over the next few months," Ann assured her. "This is our busy time of year. My department really racks up frequent flier miles."

That's what she needed, flier miles. Flying around the country, she wouldn't have time to mope about Brent. She'd be busy. Yep, she'd be much too busy to cry over Brent. Not that she was looking forward to saying good-bye to him on moving day. There was no sense kidding herself, that was going to be hard. She'd probably cry herself silly, but in the end, she'd know she'd done the right thing. And after a while, they'd both fulfill their dreams of happiness.

"Trust me, you're going to have a wonderful career at Henderson," Ann said with a smile.

A wonderful career. Yep. And travel. Fun. Excitement. Adventure.

Caitlin ignored the sadness inside and swallowed past the lump in her throat. What could be better?

Brent paced the lobby of the four-star hotel, feeling like a lion in a cage. What if coming here had been a mistake? What if Caitlin told him to buzz off? After all, if she'd wanted to talk to him, she wouldn't have left her own apartment at daybreak to head off to Dallas. Couldn't she have at least said good-bye to him before she'd left?

But she hadn't. Which ought to tell him something. Unfortunately, he was too in love to think clearly. He hadn't even hesitated about driving to Dallas as soon as his shift had ended this afternoon. He'd wanted to see Caitlin, to talk to her, and holding off a couple of days until she got back home seemed way too long.

So now he waited. Just like he had for the past two hours.

When Caitlin finally walked into the lobby, Brent cut a diagonal path through the people and reached her side just as she pushed the elevator button. Catching up to her hadn't been difficult. She was walking as if her feet hurt.

Caitlin glanced at him briefly, then with a start of recognition, smiled. "What are you doing here?"

"I came to surprise you. I hope you don't mind."

She hesitated, then leaned up on tiptoe and gave him a kiss. "I don't mind. Didn't you have to work today?"

"Just until three." He didn't know what to make of that hesitation. Was she already pulling away from him?

The elevator doors slid open, and they went inside. It was crowded, so they ended up standing close to each other. Feeling like a fifteen-year-old at the movies, Brent slowly eased his arm around her waist. When she didn't move away from his touch, he felt a surge of elation rush through him. Maybe there was hope. Maybe her disappearing act this morning hadn't been a kiss-off after all.

Then again, maybe she didn't want to cause a scene in the elevator.

A million questions crowded his mind, but he waited until they got off the elevator and headed toward her room before he asked, "How did today go?"

The brilliant smile she gave him only made him feel worse.

"It was great. Very exciting. I met a lot of people, found out I'm going to be swamped at work, even located my assigned parking space in a garage the size of a football field. And best of all, I don't think I came across as a hick."

Brent stopped walking and stared at her. "You're not a hick. What makes you say something like that?"

She laughed and tugged on his arm. "Oh, right. I'm so cosmopolitan. I've seen so much of the world."

Reluctantly, Brent moved forward at her urging. "Since when does seeing a lot of the world make you a better person? And why does staying in one place make you a hick? Personally, some days I feel like I've seen way too much of the world."

His tone made her turn her head to look at him. "You mean like when you got shot?"

"A kid on crack shot me, Caitlin. He was so out of it, he didn't even know what he'd done."

They'd reached her room. Caitlin slipped her keycard in, then pushed open the door. Once inside, she put her hand on Brent's arm.

"That kid is exactly the sort of person I'll be able to help at Henderson," she said.

"You're going to work with addicts? I admire your good intentions, Caitlin, but that could be heartbreaking. Although I can understand why you'd want to help someone turn his life around."

Caitlin released his arm and moved away. "I'm not sure yet whether I'll be helping addicts, but there are opportunities to do hands-on work here. Well, most of the time." At his questioning look, she added, "I'm going to help with fund-raising, too, so I get to travel."

That surprised him. He'd never thought Caitlin would enjoy anything like that, but what did he know? He'd thought Caitlin would at least stick around this morning to say good-bye.

"Fund-raising? Is that what you want to do?" he asked.

"My new boss thinks I'm a natural at it, and I won't be doing that much at first. Just a couple of trips a month."

"What kind of places are you going to get to visit?"

She moved over to the small sofa on the far side of the room and set down her briefcase. "Right after I start, I'm flying out to San Francisco with some other employees to attend a banquet at OptiTech.

That should be fun. I've always wanted to go to California."

She sounded overly chipper. Was she really excited about this trip or just pretending to be excited? It was difficult to tell, but he was having second thoughts about coming to Dallas. Still, he was here, so he might as well at least talk to her about his idea.

"Why don't I take you to dinner at the fanciest restaurant that will let us in?" he offered.

"I can't. Two other Henderson employees are taking me to dinner. But I can ask if you can come along."

That wasn't at all what he'd had in mind, and he shook his head. He wanted to talk to Caitlin alone.

"How much time do we have before they get here?" he asked, hoping the answer would be an hour or two.

"I'm meeting them in the bar in about five minutes. I only came back up to the room because I wanted to drop off my briefcase and change these shoes, which are killing my feet. Give me a moment, then we can head down."

Brent watched her disappear into the bathroom. So much for talking. At least for now. He'd have to wait until after dinner. With any luck, dinner would be quick.

Later, Caitlin stood in her hotel bedroom, feeling unbelievably confused. On one hand, dinner had been fun, and her soon-to-be teammates had been a hoot. Kenny had told joke after joke. And Donna was so nice and friendly that Caitlin felt as if she'd known her for years.

But on the other hand, throughout dinner, Caitlin couldn't wait to get back to the room. She wanted to be alone with Brent. No matter how much she tried to stop wanting him, the attraction was too strong. Too deep. As soon as she'd returned, she'd expected him to gather her close and make love to her. But he hadn't. Instead, he'd sat on the sofa, where he'd waited patiently through her chatty description of the dinner.

Now he sat watching her with a sort of quiet sadness. Finally he said, "So Donna says you'll be working almost nonstop for the next couple of months."

Uncertain where he was going with this, Caitlin slowly crossed the room. "That's what I understand."

"Plus doing the traveling you mentioned earlier."

Although he was making a statement rather than asking a question, she answered him anyway. "Yes, I'll be busy." What was he getting at?

He sighed and ran his hands through his hair. It was such a defeated gesture, that she ached for him.

"Caitlin, I came to see you tonight because I want to offer to move back to Dallas so we can continue to see each other. I know the last time I brought this idea up, you didn't want to talk about it, but I think we could make it work."

His offer stunned Caitlin. Brent had hated living in Dallas, yet he was willing to move back. For a fleeting moment, joy rushed through her. Then reality hit.

"When you say we could continue to see each other, what do you mean? We'd date ... or live together?"

With a rueful laugh, he said, "I was hoping we'd get married."

Married? She hadn't expected him to say that. Slowly, she walked over to the mirror above the dresser, turning the word over and over in her mind. Without really paying attention to what she was doing, she took off her earrings, setting them on the dresser in front of her. Today had been the beginning of everything she'd dreamed of for years. She should be thrilled about this job.

So why did she feel so confused? Turning to face Brent again, she asked, "Why marriage?"

"It's something a lot of people in love do. I thought it might work for us, too."

"You'd really move back here?"

"Yes," he answered simply.

Any elation she might have felt disappeared as doubt crept into her mind. Was it fair to say yes, she'd marry him, knowing he'd have to move back to Dallas, where he'd be unhappy? Worse, he'd have to spend a lot of time alone while she worked long hours at Henderson. How could she do that to him?

The tears she'd been fighting gathered in Caitlin's eyes. She was so confused. She should be happy about her new job, but she wasn't. She should be able to make up her mind about Brent, but she couldn't. Right now, Caitlin felt like nothing in her world made sense anymore.

She wanted so desperately to say yes to Brent, to tell him they could be together if he moved to Dallas, but she knew if she did, he'd end up being miserable. "Desmond is where you want to be, Brent. You've told me as much time and again."

"I've changed my mind. I'd rather be with you."

This was terrible. If she said yes, she'd make her own dreams come true but at the same time she'd destroy Brent's dreams. How could she possibly do that?

But she already knew the answer. She couldn't. There was only one solution, and as much as she hated having to do this, she had no choice. She loved Brent too much to hurt him this way.

"This won't work," she said softly. "I have to concentrate on my career. I can't also concentrate on a marriage," she said. "I've waited my whole life for this opportunity. I can't pass it up. Plus, you'd be miserable stuck in Dallas while I'm working and traveling. You'd grow to hate me, and I couldn't take that. I'm sorry, Brent."

His sigh was deep and heartfelt. "I guess I just need to accept that what we had wasn't meant to last forever." He glanced away, and Caitlin was sure he was fighting for control. When he finally looked at her, she saw pain. Raw, deep pain.

"We might as well end it now," he said. "No sense dragging this out." He stood and walked over to her, his gaze holding her own. "Caitlin, I want you to have the very best in life. You deserve it, because you're the most special woman I've ever met. And I'm glad I fell in love with you."

Before she could answer, before she could catch her breath, he gave her the tenderest of kisses and walked out the door.

Tears ran down Caitlin's cheeks unchecked, but she knew she'd done the right thing. She was absolutely certain of it. She loved Brent too much to make him unhappy. And he would be unhappy if he moved back here.

Still, it hurt. A lot. Now all she had left was her

new job. The job that was everything she'd always wanted.

Wasn't it?

Sitting on the edge of the bed, she let her tears flow. Emotions tumbled through her, one on top of the other. Anger, loneliness, pain. But mostly love. She loved Brent, but she couldn't simply walk away from the people at the Henderson Charity. She couldn't just throw all her dreams away, not now. Not when they were finally coming true. And she couldn't ask Brent to give up his dreams.

Boy, falling in love stunk. Big time. Why couldn't life be simple?

After leaving Caitlin's hotel room, Brent drove back to Desmond. By the time he reached his house, he realized the pain of leaving Caitlin was far worse than even when he'd been shot. Then, the pain had only been physical. It had hurt—hell, yes. But he'd known he would heal, that he would recover.

But he didn't feel that way now. At this moment, he felt like he'd never be happy again. Intellectually, he knew he probably would, but emotionally, he knew it would take a long time. His love for Caitlin was too deep to get over quickly.

He parked his Suburban in his garage and walked inside. Glancing around, it didn't take much effort to remember her filling these rooms with life. He wandered into his bedroom. More than likely, he'd have to get rid of that bed. Memories of their love-making would haunt him each time he tried to sleep.

She'd said that he'd hate being back in Dallas, that he wanted to be in Desmond. She was right. And she was also wrong. He wanted to be where she was. His house certainly no longer felt like a home, and he no longer felt like he belonged in Desmond. Not if Caitlin wasn't here, laughing with him, fighting with him, loving him.

He'd come back to Desmond to find a home, to belong. But his home was with Caitlin. He belonged with her. He was positive about that. Absolutely positive.

There had to be a way to change her mind. Yes, she would be busy with her new job, but that didn't matter. He could find a job, too, and he didn't have to rejoin the Dallas police force. He could be an officer in one of the surrounding suburbs. Anything just so he could be with Caitlin. Sure, she'd said she didn't think it would work. But she'd pointed out that he didn't want to live in Dallas. Could that be what was holding her back? Was she worried about him?

That would be like Caitlin. Well, whatever her motivation, he wasn't giving up on them so easily. In his heart, he knew this could work if they tried.

And he was more than willing to do his fair share of trying. Anything it took. Hell, he'd even live with her rather than ask for marriage, if that's what she wanted. Anything. Anything to bring her back into his life.

Brent grabbed his car keys off the counter and headed back to the garage. He'd just gotten home, but he could hardly wait to get to work. Since he wasn't on duty, he could spend a couple of hours seeing if he could find a job in a suburb around Dallas. Then, when Caitlin got home tomorrow, he'd tell her there wasn't anything he wouldn't do for her.

She had to understand that he couldn't imagine a life without her.

This time when he talked to her, he wasn't going to give up. She was too important. He intended to be part of her life. No doubt about it, the next time they spoke, he was going to move heaven and earth to change Caitlin's mind.

Caitlin walked slowly up the walkway to Brent's house, excitement coursing through her veins. She was doing the right thing, she just knew it.

Over the last twenty-four hours, she'd thought about her dreams, what she really wanted. What mattered to her most. It hadn't taken long for her to realize she couldn't be happy with Brent missing from her life. The dreams she'd had about leaving her home town had been made long before she'd met Brent. Long before she'd fallen in love. As she'd sat through more meetings, all she could think about was Brent. His smile. His touch. His love.

And by five o'clock yesterday, life had suddenly seemed so simple. She couldn't lose Brent. No matter what. She wanted to see him each day and love him each night. She wanted to hold their children in her arms and grow old next to him. She wanted to spend her days in Desmond with the man who meant the world to her, surrounded by her family and friends. She wouldn't be missing anything life had to offer. Rather, by being with Brent, her world would be filled with endless possibilities for happiness.

So at their breakfast meeting this morning, Caitlin had told Ann she couldn't take the job. Then she'd headed home.

To Brent.

And here she was, climbing the porch steps to Brent's house, hoping he hadn't changed his mind. She rang the doorbell and waited impatiently until she heard Brent walking to the door.

"What are you doing back?" he asked when he saw her on his doorstep. "I thought you weren't coming home until tomorrow."

He made no move to touch her, but Caitlin hadn't expected him to. "Mind if I come inside?"

Brent moved out of the doorway and waited until she was inside. Then he shut the door and turned to face her. She could feel his uncertainty, his hesitation.

"I'm surprised you stopped by," he admitted. "But I'm glad to see you."

Caitlin drew in a deep breath and went for broke. "Actually, the reason I'm here is because you're the head of Good Neighbors, and I need help."

Concern crossed his face, and he moved toward her. "Help? What's wrong? Are you all right?"

"I'm fine," she assured him. "But I've hurt the man I love, and I was hoping you could help me make things right."

For a moment, Brent looked downright stunned, and Caitlin gave him a small smile. "I drove him away because I thought we wanted different things out of life. But I know now that I was wrong. He's what I really want."

"So you want me to help you with your boyfriend?" Brent teased, and she could hear happiness in his voice. He ran his hand across his jaw, apparently considering her request. "I don't know. That kind of thing isn't something Good Neighbors usually does."

"But you do help people in need, and I really need you."

He grinned. "Really? You need me. Huh. Well, maybe I could help just a little." Moving close to her, he slipped his arms loosely around her waist. "For starters, I bet I could convince your boyfriend to move to Dallas to be with you after all."

Joy filled Caitlin. What a sweetheart. He was still willing to move for her. She lightly kissed his chin. "About that, it turns out I don't need to move to Dallas after all. I've decided to stay in Desmond." She kissed his jaw and added, "See, my boyfriend is this big yahoo on the police force, and I'm crazy about him. He mentioned marriage at one time, and I'm hoping he hasn't changed his mind. I like the idea of being married."

Brent chuckled. "Really?"

"Oh, yes."

He kissed her forehead. "Is this where the yahoo says yes?"

"I believe it is," she said, this time kissing him directly on the mouth.

The kiss was filled with passion and love and dreams of forever. When Brent lifted his head, his voice was husky as he asked, "Then the answer is yes. But what about your job?"

"I'm hoping I can find something here in town. And I'd still like to work with Good Neighbors."

"Funny thing about that. Turns out the city council has decided to fund Good Neighbors, including a salary for the director. How about that as a full-time job?"

Caitlin wasn't sure what she'd done to deserve such good fortune. "Sounds wonderful." She smiled at him.

He kissed her again, long and slow. "I love you, Caitlin. But are you absolutely certain about all of this? Staying in Desmond? Marrying me? You won't change your mind, will you?"

Caitlin laughed, anticipating the happiness to come. "No way. You're the man I love. I'm talking about forever."

Brent grinned. "Ah. My favorite word."

ABOUT THE AUTHOR

Michelle James loved to write from the moment she learned her ABCs. At age seven, she wrote her first story about eating ice cream and getting a headache. From then on, she was hooked on storytelling. After graduating with an M.A. in English, she was a technical writer for eleven years. These days, she does what she enjoys most—writing romances. To her, the best stories in the world are about love.

Michelle lives with her very supportive husband, her two great kids, and a goldfish.